A summer of football, music—and girls

"Wait!" I say. I have no idea why I say it, and I have nothing to say when she stops.

She looks at me like she's waiting for someone important.

"I went to Woodstock," I finally say.

She shrugs and smiles. "Cool." And then she goes into the locker room.

I head into the bathroom and run the water until it turns cold, then splash some on my face and wipe it off with the front of my T-shirt. I look at myself in the mirror. Feeling good.

The game-winning touchdown. And great teamwork.

I'm starting to like junior high school.

OTHER BOOKS YOU MAY ENJOY

WAR &
WATERMELON

RICH WALLACE

PUFFIN BOOKS
An Imprint of Penguin Group (USA) Inc.

PUFFIN BOOKS

Published by the Penguin Group

Penguin Young Readers Group, 345 Hudson Street, New York, New York 10014, U.S.A.

Penguin Group (Canada), 90 Eglinton Avenue East, Suite 700, Toronto, Ontario, Canada M4P 2Y3
(a division of Pearson Penguin Canada Inc.)

Penguin Books Ltd, 80 Strand, London WC2R 0RL, England

Penguin Ireland, 25 St Stephen's Green, Dublin 2, Ireland (a division of Penguin Books Ltd)

Penguin Group (Australia), 250 Camberwell Road, Camberwell, Victoria 3124, Australia
(a division of Pearson Australia Group Pty Ltd)

Penguin Books India Pvt Ltd, 11 Community Centre,
Panchsheel Park, New Delhi – 110 017, India

Penguin Group (NZ), 67 Apollo Drive, Rosedale, Auckland 0632, New Zealand
(a division of Pearson New Zealand Ltd.)

Penguin Books (South Africa) (Pty) Ltd, 24 Sturdee Avenue,
Rosebank, Johannesburg 2196, South Africa

Registered Offices: Penguin Books Ltd, 80 Strand, London WC2R 0RL, England

First published in the United States of America by Viking,
a member of Penguin Group (USA) Inc., 2011
Published by Puffin Books, a division of Penguin Young Readers Group, 2012

1 3 5 7 9 10 8 6 4 2

"Get Together"
Words and Music by Chet Powers
Copyright © 1963 IRVING MUSIC, INC.
Copyright Renewed.
All Rights Reserved. Used by Permission.
Reprinted by permission of Hal Leonard Corporation

THE LIBRARY OF CONGRESS HAS CATALOGED THE VIKING EDITION AS FOLLOWS:
Wallace, Rich.
War and watermelon / by Rich Wallace.—1st ed.
p. cm.
Summary: As the summer of 1969 turns to fall in their New Jersey town, twelve-year-old
Brody plays football in his first year at junior high while his older brother's protest
of the war in Vietnam causes tension with their father.
ISBN: 978-0-670-01152-0 (hc)
[1. Brothers—Fiction. 2. Fathers and sons—Fiction. 3. Vietnam War, 1961–1975—
Protest movements—Fiction. 4. United States—History—1969—Fiction. 5. Football—
Fiction. 6. Junior high schools—Fiction. 7. Schools—Fiction. 8. Family life—
New Jersey—Fiction. 9. New Jersey—History—20th century—Fiction.]
I. Title
PZ7.W15877War 2011
[Fic]—dc22 2010041043

Puffin Books ISBN 978-0-14-242138-3

Set in Palatino
Designed by Sam Kim

Printed in the United States of America

For my brother Bobby, the kindest person I've ever known,
and his new grandson, Tyler Robert Patrick Brady

WAR & WATERMELON

MONDAY, AUGUST 11, 1969:

Adult Swim

I look across the pool and see Patty Moriarity and Janet DeMaria hanging out by the refreshment stand. They're in two-piece bathing suits, but not bikinis. They're the type of girls that are over our heads. Not at the top of the list of coolest girls, but close to it. We're pretty much near the bottom of the guys; low-middle at best.

"Junior frickin' high school," Tony says.

We'll be starting seventh grade three weeks from tomorrow—the day after Labor Day. Switching rooms for different classes, though not as much as my brother, Ryan, did when he went there. The third floor of Franklin School was condemned last year because of the roof, but we'll still be using the rest of it. And taking shop.

We lie in the sun for about half an hour. I never tan much; I get freckles. My family is mostly Scottish, if that explains anything.

We walk past the refreshment stand, but those girls aren't

around. Gary Magrini is leaning against the bricks like he's holding up the wall. He's sneering, as always, but he gives us a slight nod of acknowledgment.

Gary's on our town's junior football team with us. He's very tan, and there are some black hairs growing around his nipples. Tony's got that dark curly hair, too, but pretty much only on his head.

I say *our* football team, but it's not mine yet. The coaches will make the final cuts tomorrow afternoon. Me and Tony are right on the cut line.

They announce an adult swim for noon—nobody under eighteen is allowed in the water for fifteen minutes.

"Let's go!" Tony says. The only time he ever wants to swim is when we're not allowed to.

We sit on the edge of the diving area with our feet dangling in the pool. It's not crowded today, so there are only about twenty adults in there. I keep my eyes on the stuck-up lifeguard with the white cream on his nose; Tony watches the chunky girl guard with the long black hair. When neither of them is looking our way, Tony whispers, "Now."

We slide off the edge and into the water, staying under as we swim toward the diving boards. We work our way behind two old guys who are hanging out near the corner. One of them has both arms over the edge of the pool and is slowly kicking his feet. The other one is bobbing up and down, keeping a hand on the wall.

We face away from the guards, out toward Route 17, and Tony starts laughing.

"What?" I ask.

"Nothing. We did it."

We've been in the water for eight seconds, so we haven't accomplished much. But anytime we get away with anything, Tony thinks it's a triumph.

We hear a whistle and I turn, but it's just the girl guard scolding a little kid for running near the pool. We sink underwater again, and I stay down for at least half a minute.

Tony was under for less time and must have burst out of the water like a drowning duck, because the other guard is already pointing at him and telling him to get out. I dive under again and swim to the other side.

I come up near the ladder and can see Tony parked on a bench behind the diving boards. The lifeguard is twirling his whistle around on its lanyard and facing Tony. He'll be benched there until the adult swim is over.

I figure I've taken enough of a risk, so I climb the ladder and shake off. I point over at Tony and give him a "ha-ha" expression, but then I feel a tap on my shoulder and the other guard is frowning at me.

"You can go join your friend on that bench," she says.

"Why?" I say, all innocent-like. I'm dripping wet, of course.

"Get moving."

"This is sweat," I say. "I was playing volleyball."

She rolls her eyes. I walk over to Tony and we crack up laughing.

Patty and Janet stroll past. We get an amused glance from Janet, whose streak of sunburn across her forehead isn't quite

3

as red as her hair. Patty is looking good, with her sun-blonde hair reaching her shoulders.

"Hey, Patty," Tony says.

She stops and looks over. She has no expression, but the way she's standing is sort of challenging. She's got a bit of muscle and some other new developments up top.

She kind of scares me. Not like she could beat me up or anything, but just that she could cut me down with a look or a few words. She could make it really clear where I stand in the eyes of girls our age. At least the popular ones. Where I stand is not very good, and we all know it.

Tony, on the other hand, does not seem to know his rank in the pecking order. He raises his hands, curving his fingers like he's holding two tennis balls. "Eee, eee," he says, squeezing the air.

Patty scowls and walks away. Janet laughs a little, then follows Patty. I punch Tony on the arm. "Idiot," I say.

He's smiling and nodding.

"Junior frickin' high school," he says again. "Can't wait for that."

There's a breeze tonight, so I throw my bedroom window open as wide as it goes. I can hear the hum of a plane landing down the hill at Teterboro Airport, and I see the red and white lights of the Empire State Building just a few miles farther to the east.

The Mets lost again. Shut out by the Astros. I can't stomach listening to the post-game, so I switch the radio over to

WMCA and catch the end of "Baby, I Love You." Then they start playing some awful Bobby Sherman song, and I'm too tired to reach over and switch to another station. So it's playing when my brother sticks his head in my room and points to the radio.

"You're still listening to that Top Forty crap?" Ryan asks.

"Still?" I got the radio three weeks ago for my twelfth birthday. How long is that? "What are *you* listening to?"

Ryan smiles. "Dylan. Hendrix. Stuff you don't hear on AM." He rubs his chin, where a scruffy blond beard is trying to establish itself. The fuzz on his face is a lot lighter than the very long strands on his head, which reach his shoulders.

My radio doesn't get FM. I fiddle with the dial and try to find another music station. The only one that comes in clear is playing the same stupid song. "Little Woman."

"Turn it up, Brody!" Ryan says. He fakes like he's really into it—miming the lyrics, swiveling his hips, and narrowing his eyes. He's lean like I am and wiry.

I switch back to the post-game. Somebody's interviewing Ron Swoboda about the Mets' slump. "Everybody's quick to blame the manager," he says. "That's too easy. We're the ones losing. The players."

Ryan laughs. "Worst team in the history of sports." He takes a seat on the edge of my bed. "Great concert coming up this weekend. Big-time scene."

"You going?"

He glances toward the door and lowers his voice. "If they

let me use the car." He's been driving for almost a year, but not often. You don't need to drive much in this town; it's not more than a mile from one end to the other. And the buses take you into the city or to Hackensack.

"Where at?"

"Upstate New York. Some farm. They say everybody's gonna be there. Jimi, Santana, Jefferson Airplane."

I don't know much about those groups, but I nod as if I do. "On a *farm*?"

"Some hippie dude's. I figure they might let me go if I take you."

"Me?" This sounds adventurous.

"Yeah. Dad will think I'll stay out of trouble if I've got you with me."

I've been getting stuck between Ryan and my dad a lot lately; they're battling about his "future," which doesn't look all that great, and there's been a lot of "tell Dad this" or "see that Ryan knows." This looks like another situation where I'll be the go-between.

"So," he says, "you up for it?"

"Saturday?"

"It's all weekend. Friday's the day I want to go. Can you skip practice?"

"Not supposed to, but maybe Mom'll write a note." I reach across to my dresser and tap on my football helmet. "I got a scrimmage Saturday afternoon."

He shrugs. "We'll be back late Friday night."

"Jenny going?"

"Of course. Skippy, too."

Jenny is his girlfriend and Skippy is a delinquent who lives next door to her and has been her best friend for a long time. Skippy tags along with them everywhere they go. They don't seem to mind. Ryan never had a lot of close friends, so when he acquired Jenny last spring, he got two for one. That changed things for him and me kind of abruptly—I had Ryan to myself most of the time before that. Jenny's sweet, but she's with him every spare minute.

Ryan picks up a G.I. Joe from my dresser and looks at it. I've outgrown those things; just haven't gotten around to throwing them out yet. "There's like a hundred bands gonna be there," he says. "Or maybe fifty. I don't know—a lot."

"You ain't working?"

Ryan stocks the frozen food shelves at Shop-Rite. Full-time since he graduated from high school in June. Our parents are pissed off that he didn't even apply to college. Especially with the draft and everything.

"I'm calling in," he says. "Twenty-four-hour virus." He leans over with his mouth open and makes a puking sound. He laughs. "It's going around."

I can hear our parents coming up the stairs to go to bed. They stop at my door. "Keep it low, guys, all right?" Dad says.

"I gotta shower anyway," Ryan says, meaning he's about to leave the room. He usually leaves whatever room he's in as soon as Dad appears.

I turn the volume way down.

Ryan stands up. "You don't need the car Friday afternoon, do you?" he asks.

"Well, I don't know," Mom says. "Were you thinking of going to the mall?"

"I was wanting to go to this . . . musical event. Friday evening. Brody wants to go, so I thought I'd take him."

"Oh." Mom smiles. "That sounds nice."

"Great," he says. "So it's okay?"

"Well, probably. Where is it?"

Ryan gazes out the window. "It's in New York."

Mom looks horrified. "Then take the bus."

"Upstate."

"Oh . . . I don't know then." She shifts her eyes to Dad. "That's so far."

"No," Ryan says. "It's like an hour. Less than two. It's right off the Thruway."

The more he talks, the less likely it is that they'll let him go. Come *on*, Mom! This is gonna be great.

"Ryan, I don't know," Mom says. "You'd be gone a long time and would end up driving in the dark."

"I've driven in the dark plenty."

"Yes, but close to home."

"I can handle it."

Mom folds her arms across her chest, but I can tell she wants to let him down easy. "There's a dance right here at the swim club on Friday night. Why don't you go to that instead? They'll be playing rock and roll, I'm sure."

"Mom. Janis Joplin's gonna be there. Arlo Guthrie. That's not exactly what you get at a swim club dance."

She sighs and turns to my dad. "What do you think, Alex?" When she does that, it means she's made up her mind. She just throws it over to Dad to make it unanimous.

But he stuns us all. "I think Ryan can handle it. There wouldn't be much traffic on a Friday afternoon."

Ryan makes two fists and goes into a flex. "All right, Dad," he says. "Solid!"

Mom frowns but goes along with it. "You take good care of Brody," she says.

Dad lets out his breath and his lips vibrate. He's mostly bald, and his head is shiny by the end of the day. He lifts one eyebrow and peers over at Ryan. "Think about filling out that application to Drew," he says. "We can get you in for the second semester."

So that's the trade-off: apply to college. Ryan turns eighteen next month. Eligible for the draft. Old enough to get killed in Vietnam.

Ryan rolls his eyes, but he knows this is no time to argue. "Okay," he says. "Like you said, I'll *think* about it."

The four of us look back and forth at each other for a few seconds. Ryan says thanks again, then heads for the bathroom. Mom kisses me on the cheek and turns off my light.

I lie there for a couple of hours, listening to the Top Forty on the radio and the crickets out on the lawn. I imagine myself taking a handoff at midfield, dodging right, and bursting through the line. A defender gets a hand on me, but I shake loose and pivot, cutting toward the sideline and stiff-arming a linebacker. They're all chasing me now, and I tuck the ball tight to my chest and open my stride, dashing untouched to the end zone and lifting the ball high in the air.

Sometime after midnight I fall asleep.

At 4:39 I wake up to the Archies singing "Sugar, Sugar." It's already getting light out and the birds are chirping, but there's no way I'm starting my day this early. I shut the window, turn off the music, and climb back into bed.

The Archies are comic-book characters. What the heck are they doing on my radio?

And why isn't Ryan doing everything he can to keep from getting drafted? It's not like he can stop the calendar from turning just by ignoring it.

Taylor Ham

My dad is up every morning by five thirty, eating stale cake and strong coffee and using the bathroom in the cellar three or four times. He listens to *Rambling with Gambling* on the radio and reads the *New York Times* before heading out the door to catch the 6:25 bus at the corner.

For eleven and a half years I was basically unaware of his early morning routine, but midway through the last school year I began spending a couple of minutes with him before he left for the city. Right after his father died. It's important to spend that time together, just the two of us, even though we hardly say a thing.

Today the radio's going on about the war.

"Gideon?" Dad says as I walk into the kitchen, pretending that he's surprised to see me. (He calls me a different name every morning.) He's got his dress shoes and pants on, but up top he's just wearing a guinea T. There's a tiny square of bloody toilet paper on his jaw where he nicked himself shaving.

"Hey," I say, opening the refrigerator.

"Mets lost last night."

"I heard it. They're like eight games behind already." They suck again, like every year.

Two weeks ago it looked like the Mets would be taking over first place. Nobody thought they'd do anything this season, but they stayed close to the Cubs for most of the summer. Now they're falling apart.

"They made a good run," he says. "Maybe next year."

"Maybe." Maybe next century.

Dad nods slowly, chewing. "Eat something?" he asks.

I shrug. There's a box of doughnuts on the counter, but they're those white powdered ones that I can't stand. "Maybe toast," I say.

"How's Ferrante's arm looking?" he asks. Tommy Ferrante is our quarterback. We know him from when I was in Cub Scouts, but he quit that in fourth grade and became a borderline crook. The only real use of his arm that I know of is when he and Magrini got caught throwing rocks off the cliff to bust windows at a warehouse.

"It's okay, I guess. We never pass anyway. Ninety-nine plays out of a hundred are handoffs."

"You getting any of them?"

"Nah. They mostly put me at linebacker." I've carried twice in scrimmages so far. Both times I got nailed for lost yardage.

Dad pours another cup of coffee, looks at the clock, and chugs it. The empty cup is still steaming when he sets it down.

He told me once that he drinks at least twenty-five cups of coffee a day, virtually nonstop, at the office.

He goes upstairs to finish dressing and I move into his seat at the counter. The *Times* headline says, "Enemy Attacks 100 Vietnam Sites."

I'm eating a doughnut anyway when he comes back in his suit jacket and a blue tie. He combed his hair, basically pasting the few long strands from one side over his scalp with Vitalis. He kisses the top of my head, then hesitates. "Make sure your brother sees that Vietnam headline," he says. "This isn't Little League. He can't just take the pitch and hope for the best."

He picks up his briefcase and heads out the door. I go to the window and watch him walk very upright and swiftly along the sidewalk. I feel sad for a minute every morning when he slips out of sight for the next twelve hours. Mom says his health has never been too good, that he might need a pacemaker in a few years.

I can't believe he brought up the Little League thing again. Ryan swears Dad's obituary will read that his only regret was that his son struck out looking.

Here's how I've heard it explained over the years. I was three when it happened, so I have no recollection.

Dad's coaching. Ryan is up to bat in an important game. It's the classic baseball situation: bottom of the last inning, two outs, bases loaded, his team down by a run. A single wins

13

the game, but even a walk brings in a run and sets things up for the next guy.

So the count is three balls and two strikes, or maybe two balls and two strikes. Either way, you have to swing at a strike, no matter how hard you're praying it'll be called a ball. The pitch is straight over the plate, waist-high, but Ryan freezes. He doesn't swing.

Strike three.

Allegedly, the bitter aftermath of all that is why Mom wouldn't let Dad coach *my* Little League teams. And why Ryan opted out of every sport except basketball, with the stip-ulation that Dad not attend any of the games.

In my first baseball game, I struck out three times. But I swung at all nine pitches. Dad made a big point of saying how proud he was that I went down swinging. That I "showed some heart out there."

He said that in front of Ryan, of course. He still brings it up every once in a while, thinking he's being subtle.

I watch a Bugs Bunny cartoon—the one where Elmer Fudd's uncle Louie died—then a Daffy Duck and another Bugs. When my mother wakes up, she fries some Taylor Ham, and I eat that and a bowl of Cocoa Krispies.

"Brody, you don't have to go to this concert with your brother on Friday if you don't want to," she says. "We'll let him use the car even if you stay home."

"I want to go."

"All right. But you don't have to."

"I know, but it'll be a blast."

"Well," she says, pouring coffee into Dad's cup for herself, "you *do* get carsick."

"Ryan says it isn't far."

"Ryan says a lot of things." She sips the coffee, then sets down the cup and sweeps powdered sugar off the counter with one hand, catching it in the other. "He's a sweet boy, but he's as naive as they come. And they don't give you any breaks for being sweet in the army."

My knee's bleeding, just a trickle below the cap where it jabbed into a stone as I tried to tackle Kenny Esposito. I was *on* my knees at the time, not exactly the best tackling posture, and when I reached for him I twisted sideways and was knocked farther back by *his* knee hitting my shoulder.

"You gotta put your weight into that tackle," an assistant coach said to me with a snarl. "You can't do that from your knees, man."

"I got knocked down."

"Don't *get* knocked down," he said, spraying out the words.

My weight: 87 pounds. Esposito weighs at least 120. He scored on the next play, barreling through the line and virtually carrying Tony and another guy with him as they tried to bring him down.

That was an hour ago, before I made a couple of actual tackles and before the wind sprints and the long laps around the field at the end of practice.

That coach acted like a jerk, but it stung.

Despite all that, I made the team. First time trying out, too. They sent Johnny Rivera home for good, which surprised the heck out of me. He's fast and he played hard, but he's new in town and Puerto Rican, so in the coaches' eyes he's suspect.

The rest of the cuts were eleven-year-olds.

So I'm in. I don't think I'll get a lot of playing time, but the point is that I made it. I'm basically lost in that crowd, hanging on as one of the least important players.

Now me and Tony are walking home, carrying our helmets by the face masks with our cleats stuffed inside.

"That field is a killer," Tony says, examining the bloody spot on his elbow. He's no bigger than I am.

"It's like the Sea of Tranquility," I say. The astronauts landed on that area of the moon a couple of weeks ago. We watched it in the family room with all the shades drawn and the air conditioner on high. "One small step for man . . ."

I was in the bathroom when Neil Armstrong actually stepped onto the lunar surface. Diarrhea.

"They've landed!" my mom yelled.

"I know!" I yelled back.

"He's coming out of the rocket ship!"

I can't move from this spot, I thought. Maybe I actually said it, but not loud enough that anybody but me could have heard. Especially through the bathroom door.

"This is a once-in-a-*life*time thing, Brody!"

So is this food poisoning, I hope. Mom had made chicken

salad for the occasion. It sat on the picnic table all afternoon before I ate it.

"In here?" Tony asks, jutting his thumb toward the doorway at Fisher's. We usually grab a can of soda on the long walk home from practice. Plus it's air-conditioned in there, so we get to cool off for a minute.

I set my helmet on the sidewalk and wriggle a finger into my sneaker, but I can't reach the two quarters I stashed there. So I step on the heel with my other sneaker and pry my foot out. The quarters are wedged up by the toes.

"Those'll be real pleasant to handle," Tony says.

"That's why I took them out here. They probably wouldn't accept them if they saw where I kept 'em."

Tony smirks. "You might as well store 'em in your cup."

We grab drinks and stare at the magazine rack for a few seconds. Tony looks around, then carefully peels back the upper corner of a *Playboy* cover, trying to get a peek inside.

"Hey!" says the guy behind the counter.

"Just looking," says Tony, quickly stepping away. He gives me an embarrassed grin. We've seen pictures like that before.

Just looking. That's been the story of our lives.

Misunderstanding All You See

Ryan knocks on my door, which is open, then steps in. "You wanna hear something cool?" he asks. He's wearing a baggy Giants jersey with the sleeves torn off, so you can see his entire bony arms.

"Sure." I reach over and turn off my radio. "What?"

"In my room. This is really freaky."

We go in and shut his door tight. The black light is on; the Day-Glo posters are shimmering. Skippy is sitting on Ryan's desk with the window wide open, looking squirrely and blowing smoke out through the screen. I can see lightning bugs hovering over the yard in the darkness.

Jenny gives me a big smile. She dyed her hair blonde this summer, and it's pulled back in a long ponytail. I get the impression that she was one of the cool ones back in junior high school, but she's really nice now. She graduated from high school with Ryan a couple of months ago.

Ryan holds up a Beatles album cover—*Magical Mystery Tour*. "Hello Goodbye" is playing on the record player.

The next song comes on. "Just listen," Ryan says.

"They say Paul McCartney is dead," Skippy says, flicking some ashes into a Coke bottle. You can tell he hasn't spent five seconds in the sun this summer; his skin is as pale as an eggshell.

"Who says?"

"People. They're trying to hide it, but there's like a million clues in this record."

It's a hundred degrees in here, but Skippy is still wearing his black leather jacket.

"Who's trying to hide it?"

"The Beatles," he says. "But they gave it away."

Ryan puts up his hand for quiet. We listen to "Strawberry Fields Forever" until that weird instrumental ending comes on. Ryan turns it to full volume and says, "Everybody shut up."

When the song has nearly faded to silence, you hear this faint, moany voice saying something like "Ah bwuwy bawwwww."

"You hear that?" Ryan says.

"I heard something," I reply.

"He said, 'I buried Paul.' That was John Lennon."

"He couldn't hold the secret any longer," Skippy says.

"Oh." I look at Ryan. I think he can tell I'm doubtful.

"There's lots of other clues," Ryan says.

"Like what?"

"If you play some of these songs backwards there's all sorts of stuff that comes through," he says excitedly.

"Can you do that?" I ask, my interest rising.

Ryan stares at the record player for a few seconds. He shrugs. "I guess not," he says. "But somebody did it. They have proof."

I nod. "Oh."

"Look at the names of these songs," Skippy says, pointing to the album cover. "'I Am the Walrus.' You know what being a walrus means?"

"No."

"It's a symbol for death in some Eskimo language or something. So Paul's basically saying, 'I am dead.'"

"Why would he say that?"

"Because he *is*."

Ryan tries to clarify things. "He sang it before he was dead."

Skippy gets a smug look on his face and points at me with his cigarette. "But now he is. Dead, I mean."

I go back to my room and listen to the last inning of the Mets game, then sit through nine songs on WMCA before "Get Together" finally comes on. ("Come on people now . . .")

The Mets lost again. Third straight to the Astros. I don't know why I bother listening. They just kill you. I can't sleep, so I go downstairs around midnight to get a drink and find Ryan in the kitchen with the bottles of food coloring on the counter.

"You making Easter eggs?" I ask. I'm serious; that's the only thing we've ever used that stuff for.

"Watch this," he says. He holds up a white T-shirt and spreads it over the sink. Then he picks up the red bottle and squeezes a few drops onto the shirt. He takes the green one and holds it a bit higher. "Got to make it splash a little."

When he's finished with the yellow and blue bottles, he holds up the shirt. "Tie-dye," he says. "At least it looks like tie-dye . . . kind of."

He takes the shirt into the cellar and I follow him. We've got a clothesline down there, reaching from above my dad's workbench to a hook above the washing machine. He hangs the shirt there, and a few drops of blue and red drip onto the cement floor.

"Should be good to go for the concert," he says. "You been hearing who's gonna be there? Canned Heat. The frickin' Grateful Dead. They even think Dylan might show up, but you can never count on him."

Bob Dylan I've heard of, but not most of the other groups Ryan's been going on about the past few days. Still, I am definitely looking forward to this. Just hanging out with Ryan at a thing like that will be awesome.

"Total peacefest," he says. "Music and revolution."

He picks up a green rubber ball—maybe half the size of a basketball—bounces it once, then shoots it at the hoop we've got nailed to the wall. The ceiling is only six and a half feet high, so it's tough to do anything but dunk the ball. We used to play one-on-one basketball down here for hours at a time.

The thing is, as far as I can remember, Ryan was just as much of a dweeb as I am. He didn't get cool until recently. I think he knows where I'm at in life, because he's been there. So he includes me in a lot of things, but it's never just me and him anymore.

The hoop is a miniature, half as wide as a real one. It's got a bell attached beneath the rim that's supposed to ring anytime a basket is made. The bell works maybe 10 percent of the time.

We've got a piece of electrical tape on the floor about two feet from the opposite wall, for the backcourt, so there's about a nine-by-nine area for game action. Fouls are legal, unless you actually grab your opponent or draw blood. That happens a lot.

It's also legal to pass to yourself by bouncing the ball off any wall.

Ryan beats me two straight: 20–12 and 20–16. We're laughing and making quite a bit of noise with the passes off the wall and the dribbling and the grunting.

We hear the cellar door being yanked open, then Dad's voice. "Creepin' Jeebus! What is going on down there?"

"Playing basketball," I reply.

"It's one o'clock in the morning!"

"I'm not tired."

"Is Ryan down there with you?"

We look at each other. Ryan breaks into a grin and says, "Yeah."

"You're both out of your minds," Dad says. "Get some sleep. So *I* can." He shuts the door hard.

Ryan hands me the ball. "Game point," he says. "For the title."

I take two dribbles, make a big step to the left, then dodge under his arm and leap for the basket. He gets a hand on the ball and knocks it toward the furnace. "That's out," I say.

I grab the ball, make a juke to the right, and send a line drive over the clothesline and directly into the basket. The bell rings. Ryan puts his hands on his hips and stares at the ceiling. I raise my fists and say, "Yes!"

I carefully move past the shirt—it looks more like polka dots than tie-dye—and smack hands with him. "Champion," I say, patting myself on the chest.

"Mr. Clutch," he says. "Best in the basement, for sure."

Sugar and Speed

The cheerleaders are practicing at the same time we are today, so we keep looking over at them. Most of them have boyfriends on the team.

"We should sleep out soon," says Tony, standing behind me. We're in line for a pass-catching drill.

We do that a few times every summer, pitching a tent in the yard and stuffing our faces with candy all night. Last time, he brought a cigar from his father's stash, and we both nearly puked after taking a few puffs.

"No more smokes," I say.

"No. Maybe a bucket of chicken, though."

The cheerleaders are doing their basic introductory cheer, going through the names of the players. I know they do a cheer for every guy on the team, and that the names come up alphabetically, but I still get kind of a chill when I hear Stephie Jungerman doing my name. Tony smacks me on the arm and I blush, listening to Stephie.

"Rah Brody Winslow!"

"Hey hey!"

"Rah *Brody*, rah *Winslow*, rah rah Brody Winslow!"

As it turns out, it's my turn to run a pass route the second the cheer ends. I take four quick steps, make a juke to the left, then turn to the right for the ball.

Ferrante's thrown it way inside, and I reach back for it. It smacks off my shoulder pad and rolls to the dirt.

I go to pick it up and I knock it with my foot, and it wobbles about five yards away.

"Nice coordination!" somebody yells.

I pick up the ball and toss it back, then trot to the end of the line.

"She got to ya, huh?" Tony says as he gets in place behind me. He made a great catch, tipping an overthrow and diving for it.

"No way," I say. I glance over at Stephie, sixty yards away. "Like she even knows who I am."

"She's got your name," he says.

"Yeah, and about fifty other ones. Including Gary."

"Nice math," Tony says. "They only have four or five names each."

I give him a shove. "Alphabetical," I say.

"Fate!" he replies. "That's why Marianne got *my* name."

"Don't hold your breath, man. You wouldn't make her top twenty."

"Oh, like you would?"

"Not likely."

It's true that none of the cheerleaders would even know who I am. I don't even know if *I* know who I am.

I finally get a chance to play some offense near the end of the scrimmage session, going in at tailback. Tony's at fullback. Joey Salinardi is taking the snaps; he's a year younger and probably won't play much in the games unless Ferrante gets hurt or we have some blowouts.

Coach Epstein is calling the plays. He drives a delivery truck for Wonder Bread, so he starts his days even earlier than my dad, which makes him available for our practices at three thirty.

"Okay, mini-backs, let's move the ball," Coach says, hands on his knees and froth in the corners of his mouth. "Forty-two on two."

We clap our hands, break the huddle, and line up. Forty-two means a handoff to me between the center and the right guard. I'll be following Tony through the hole, if there is one.

I try to stay steady, not looking toward the hole. Joey takes the snap and immediately drops the ball. It takes an odd bounce right off its tip. Tony dives on it and covers it up.

Coach shakes his head as we huddle up. "You gotta have the ball before you try to give it away, Joey. Run it again. On three."

I'm less tense already. Somebody else screwed up before I got the chance to.

Joey fakes to Tony and I come charging up, head down,

wrapping my arms around the ball. Tony gets knocked backward and I dodge so he'll miss me. There's no place to run. I cut to my right and am met head-on by Magrini. I hug the ball as I go down.

Loss of two yards, at least.

"Where's my blockers?" Coach says. Brian Finken is at right guard, and he got swamped. "Thirty-one this time." That's Tony to the other side.

Tony gets to the line of scrimmage and no farther.

"Let's open it up a little," Coach says.

"Can I pass?" Joey asks.

"I don't know. Can you?" Coach smiles. "Let's keep it on the ground. Forty-six pitch." He looks at me and nods, wiping his mouth with his wrist, then turns to Joey. "Fake it to Tony going off the other guard first."

The fake to Tony pulls the defense in that direction, and Joey flips the ball to me on the run. Magrini's already in the backfield, but I dodge inside him and sprint past the line of scrimmage. The only guy in front of me is Kenny Esposito, playing cornerback.

I cut toward the sideline, running as hard as I can, and race upfield. Esposito's got an angle on me and brings me down hard, but I pop right up and jog back to the huddle.

"Twelve yards!" Tony says, smacking my hands.

My breath is coming in short little bursts, and my heart is beating like crazy. Salinardi whacks my helmet and says, "Nice run!"

Coach calls another handoff to Tony. As we break the huddle, I hear Tony whispering, "Rah rah Brody Winslow!"

"Honky Tonk Women" has taken over the number-one spot on the charts, so they're playing it at least twice an hour. I can agree with that, but here's my own top five for the week:

- "Get Together" (meaningful)
- "A Boy Named Sue" (hilarious)
- "Honky Tonk Women" (rocking)
- "Sweet Caroline" (mellow)
- "In the Year 2525" (eeeerie)

These are the worst:

- "Crystal Blue Persuasion" (nauseating)
- "Sugar, Sugar" (I hate chewing bubblegum and I hate listening to it.)
- "Little Woman" (Don't even ask.)

I couldn't sleep even if I wanted to. It's humid, but that's not it. I keep thinking about that run, the way the hole opened up and I saw the entire field in front of me. How I raced past the defenders and would have scored if Esposito hadn't had the perfect angle.

It feels like my whole life's about to change. Moving into junior high is like stepping out of childhood, whether you want to or not. And I keep worrying about how much longer my brother will be around, and maybe my father, too, and wondering why they can't see eye to eye about anything this summer.

There's enough light coming in from the streetlight that I can study the cracks on my ceiling. It's like looking at cloud formations. There's one pattern that looks like a baby alligator sitting on the back of a bigger alligator. You have to use some imagination to see it, but it's there.

There's another spot that looks like a football player stretching to catch the ball. That one's a lot more abstract than the alligators. It never dawned on me that it looked like a football player until I saw some paintings in a magazine a few years ago.

See, Ryan has always been a huge Giants fan. He and my father watch every away game on TV and listen to the home games on the radio. Ryan has kept a Giants scrapbook for years. It's mostly clippings from sports magazines, but he also has some old stuff like game programs from the 1940s that belonged to my father's father.

Anyway, one day when I was seven, I found a magazine on the counter and it had paintings of some of the Giants. It wasn't a sports magazine; it was *Time* or *Life* or something like that. The paintings weren't very detailed—just bright colors and wide strokes—but they looked so active.

I figured Ryan would love to have them for his scrapbook, so I cut them out. I did a very crappy job of it, too.

A while later I'm in my room and I hear Ryan yell, "Who cut up my magazine?"

I brought the pictures downstairs and said, "I cut out the Giants for you."

"Oh," he said. I could tell he was fighting back something—tears or anger, maybe—but he stayed quiet for a minute. Then he took the pictures and went up to his room.

Later he called me over and showed me how he'd retrimmed the pictures and carefully pasted them in the scrapbook. "They look even better here than they did in the magazine," he said.

They didn't, and we both knew it. But the thing is, he didn't get mad at me. At least, he didn't show me that he was mad. He's *never* said a harsh word to me. Not once in my entire life.

FRIDAY, AUGUST 15:

Town's End

The concert is scheduled to start at four. Ryan's so psyched for it that he yells up the stairs right after lunch. "Brody! We should split."

He's wearing his homemade tie-dye shirt and a red headband.

I look in my dresser and find my old blue and yellow Cub Scout neckerchief. I tie it around my head. Freaky!

"You fellas make sure you put on plenty of suntan lotion," Mom says.

"Have you looked outside?" Ryan asks. "Nothing but clouds."

"Well, it won't hurt to bring some with you. I packed sandwiches and oranges. Do you want to take this watermelon?"

The watermelon is huge; it probably weighs twenty-five pounds.

Ryan laughs. "Why would we bring a watermelon?"

"It can be very refreshing. I bet you'll be glad you brought it."

Ryan rolls his eyes. "Okay."

Mom is filling the red and white Coleman juice dispenser with Tang and ice cubes.

"Mom, we're not lugging that thing to the concert."

She gives Ryan a look that says she knows better. "You'll thank me later. It isn't heavy—two gallons. Brody can carry it."

By the time we pick up Jenny and Skippy it's nearly two o'clock. The thing is, we have to drop off an apple pie at Aunt Lizzie's house in Port Jervis, New York, which is out of the way but in the general direction of the concert. So we'll be going on back roads instead of taking Route 17 and the New York Thruway. I think the only reason we're dropping off the pie is so Aunt Lizzie can give us directions and report back to Mom that we're halfway to our destination.

Lizzie is my grandmother's sister. "She knows every road in that area," Mom says. "She'll send you to White Lake the safest way, and she'll also know where you can stop to go to the bathroom."

Skippy smokes eight cigarettes before we even get to Port Jervis. I'm in the backseat with him, in my family's red Plymouth station wagon. No air conditioner and a radio that gets only AM.

Jenny spends most of the time turned toward us, talking about how exciting this trip is and how her all-time favorite, Joan Baez, is supposed to be performing tonight. Jenny's wearing a silver chain with a small peace sign hanging from it, and she wove some tiny reddish flowers into her hair. "This is wild," she says. "We probably won't get home until one o'clock in the morning!"

"I heard there's gonna be sixty thousand people at this thing," Ryan says, drumming his fingers on the dashboard. "Sly and the Family Stone tonight!"

I've only vaguely heard of these performers, but I'm excited. We catch bits and pieces of news on the radio, but the reception is terrible. Lots of concert-related traffic up ahead, they're saying, but so far we haven't hit any.

"Rolling Stones gonna be at this thing?" I ask when "Honky Tonk Women" comes on the radio.

"Doubt it," Ryan says.

"How 'bout the Archies?"

Everybody laughs at that one.

That's another thing about Ryan and Jenny: They laugh when I try to be funny. Tony's the only other person who ever laughs at my jokes, especially if they're about snot or farting.

"It's not just the music," Ryan says. "The way they've been talking about this on the radio stations, you just know it's going to change the way things are in this country. You get sixty thousand people protesting about Vietnam—and doing it with peace and brotherhood—then those idiots in Washington will know they'd better start listening to our generation. That's what this is all about: bringing down the establishment."

That's not what Dad said. He told me to stick within an arm's length of Ryan every second and expect to see a crowd "full of damn fools getting stoned."

Aunt Lizzie has made a huge pot roast. She lives alone and we see her only once or twice a year. No way she could finish all that meat herself, so we sit at her dining room table for an hour and a half, eating beef and potatoes and most of the pie that my mother sent.

"You'll turn onto Route 55 in a few miles, and that'll take you all the way to White Lake," she says for the tenth time as we're leaving. "You can't miss it."

It's 5:07 when we get under way again, but Aunt Lizzie assures us we'll be there in less than an hour.

We pass lots of cows and barns and pine trees. Traffic starts to build. After an hour Ryan picks up four hitchhikers—two guys and two girls around his age with backpacks. One of the guys has a guitar. They've got a handmade sign that says WOODSTOCK in big red letters.

The two guys get in the third seat by the watermelon—the seat that faces backward—and the girls squeeze between me and Skippy.

The one next to me says her name is Annie. She's skinny and smells strongly of armpit. She has long, straight brown hair and keeps giggling. The other girl is even skinnier and has a woven headband with a hand-rolled cigarette stuck in it over her ear.

They say they started out on Tuesday from Grand Rapids, Michigan. "Haven't brushed our teeth since then," says one of the guys with a laugh.

"I have," says Annie. She shows me her teeth. "Yesterday."

"Okay if we light up?" says the girl next to Skippy.

"Sure," says Ryan. "Just keep the windows open."

The cigarette she lights is obviously not tobacco. I've never smelled it before, but I'm not stupid. It's pot. Skippy and Jenny take drags on it, but Ryan says not while he's driving.

Skippy reaches across the girls and tries to hand it to me, but I shake my head. I catch Ryan's eyes in the rearview mirror. "No way," he says to Skippy. "Keep that thing away from him."

Not like I was tempted. "Anybody want Tang?" I ask.

"Absolutely," says Annie.

I realize right away that we don't have any cups. So I hold the cooler up, stick my mouth under the nozzle, and push the button to get a direct squirt. It's basically orange-colored sugar water—fortified with Vitamin C! We pass the dispenser around the car, and everybody takes hits from it.

Traffic continues to build, and the reports on the radio say that the concert crowd is already way bigger than anyone expected. We figured we'd get tickets at the gate, but I'm starting to wonder if we'll get in at all. The people running the show actually issued a radio alert telling anybody still on the road to turn back, but no way we're stopping. I mean, these hitchhikers have been on the road for three days to get to this thing. The van ahead of us is from Maryland, and the car behind us has Ohio plates and is packed to the gills with hippies. Everybody's moving in one direction, but very slowly now.

I feel a surge of nervous energy thinking about it. Hippies and dancing and rock music and me! Biggest event of my life, for sure. Let's get there!

After another hour the car is moving only about twenty feet a minute because of the traffic. As we come to the top of a hill we can see an endless stream of vehicles ahead of us. Most of the cars are parked along the shoulders, and there are people walking on both sides of the road.

"Are we there?" I ask.

"Doubt it," Ryan says. "We must be getting close, though."

We inch forward for another few minutes, and then we're at a standstill. Ryan keeps the car running, but we all get out. The male hitchhikers step into the woods to take a leak. Jenny and the two girls stand near the back of the car and start laughing at them, because they're barely off the road. I follow Ryan as he walks toward a group standing by another car.

"We close?" he asks.

"It's probably two miles to 17B," a fat guy with a huge beard says. "Most people are hoofing it from here."

"How far when we get to 17B?"

The guy shrugs. "Not much. Maybe another mile."

Ryan looks at me. "Up for a three-mile walk?"

"What?" I say, like it's no big deal. "You're talking to a *football* player here. I can take anything."

We walk back to the car and Ryan pulls it off the road, lining it up behind a brown van with Pennsylvania plates and a STOP THIS IMMORAL WAR bumper sticker. "Good a place as any," he says.

I glance at Ryan's watch. It's five minutes to eight. We're a long way from Bergen County, New Jersey, that's for sure.

We all start walking. I carry the jug of Tang and Ryan takes the bag of sandwiches. Skippy and Jenny grab the flashlights.

Soon the four of us are a hundred yards ahead of the hitch-hikers. Skippy keeps looking back. "Neither one of them was wearing a bra," he says.

"They're totally stoned," Ryan says. He glances at Jenny and smiles. "Don't get any ideas about taking yours off," he says. "I don't want nobody looking at you but me."

There are *lots* of people to look at. I haven't seen anybody near my age; most of them are older than Ryan. There's gotta be five hundred people within sight, all walking in the same direction. The sun isn't down yet, but it's definitely getting darker. The woods on both sides of the road are full of tall, thick evergreens. We walk between the stopped cars right down the middle of the road, which is a two-laner. I feel important just being here; this event will be huge.

We take a break around nine fifteen, leaning against a red Mustang from Ontario and eating oranges from the bag. We've walked way more than the two miles that fat guy said it'd be. I'm already thinking about how late we're going to get home tonight.

Skippy says his feet are sore. "Any of you know how much

farther?" he calls to a group of three guys walking with cans of Schaefer beer.

One guy in a leather cowboy hat puts his hand to his ear and says, "I think I hear Jimi wailing." Then he laughs. He points forward with his beer can. "Right around the bend, I believe."

It's dark now, so we walk closer together and shine the flashlights at the road. The guy was almost right—we reach 17B in about thirty more minutes.

Cars are everywhere; not just in the road and on the shoulders, but up in cornfields and down in ditches. "How many people are going to this thing?" Ryan asks, shaking his head.

"Millions," Skippy says. "We must have walked fifty miles. I'm out of cigarettes."

"Now *that's* an emergency," Jenny says. "Skippy without a butt. Think you'll survive?"

"I'll bum some at the concert," he says. "Where is it?"

"We ain't there yet," says a woman walking behind us. She's wearing a peace-sign necklace and a long skirt. She waves up the road. "It's another couple of miles."

"This is insane," Skippy says.

We walk along the edge of 17B. At least it's mostly flat here. After ten more minutes I say to hold up. That Tang's made its way through me. I take a flashlight from Jenny and duck into a gate, where a sign says EVERGREEN CEMETERY.

I decide I've carried the cooler long enough and I'll just pick it up on the way back. So I ditch it behind the gravestone of Johnny Townsend. It says he died on May 26, 1889. I like that name—Town's End. I feel like I've walked through the world's longest town.

"Does this concert go all night?" I ask Ryan when I get back to the road.

"I don't know. It goes late. We'll catch a ride back to the car when it's over."

"*Sure* we will," says Jenny. She yawns. We hear a low rumble of thunder and start walking again.

We pass a white wooden church packed with people. Light is shining from the stained-glass windows. There's a bonfire in the dirt parking lot, and some hippies are dancing around it.

In about twenty minutes we start to hear music way in the distance and we feel a few drops of rain. We turn onto a dirt road and start moving faster.

"That's Ravi Shankar, I bet," Ryan says.

Never heard of him, but I get a chill anyway. Must be significant if Ryan thinks so. The music sounds tinny and weird to me, but we're still a good distance away.

The rain becomes steady, then turns into a downpour. But the air is warm and we're overheated from walking so far, so it feels good. I can smell wood smoke and swamp.

We reach the top of a hill and there's this huge valley below us, and it's absolutely filled with people. Unbelievable. There's a stage way down at the far end throwing light onto the hill. People are sliding down the muddy slope on their butts. Everybody is dancing and spinning and yelling.

"Jesus," Ryan whispers. "We made it."

We just stand there with our mouths hanging open, staring at the throng of people packed shoulder to shoulder on every inch of the hill. Even in the partial darkness, I can tell that there has to be *way* more than sixty thousand here. That's about how many you'd get at a Mets game, and this crowd looks like it would fill Shea Stadium more than twice over. Everybody seems to have long hair and bare feet and scruffy dungarees and peace signs and headbands and tie-dye shirts. That is, if they're wearing shirts at all. A lot of people aren't.

The crowd is waving their arms and chanting, "No rain! No rain!" between songs, but it's coming down in buckets. It's dripping down my face, and my sneakers are full of mud. I join in—"No rain!"—but who cares? Let it come down. I start laughing for no reason. Just happy.

We make our way down the hill; there's no sign of a ticket booth. It hasn't been raining long, but the grass is already slick. It smells like cow manure.

The closer we get to the stage, the denser the crowd, but there are flashes of lightning, so some people head for cover. We get to within twenty yards of the stage. There are people sitting in the mud with pretty much all of their clothes off, smoking marijuana and laughing. You hear lots of shouting about the war between songs. About ending it.

The guy onstage is singing a sort of familiar song, saying how he sees the morning light after staying up till dawn.

"Yeah!" Ryan yells. "That'll be us in the morning."

"We'll be dead meat in the morning," I say, but I don't care. Ryan is part of this thing, part of the reason for it, part of this throng that doesn't want to kill or be killed for that immoral war. I'm not even sure what *immoral* means, but it isn't good.

There's no place I'd rather be than in this muddy field with him.

Ryan laughs. "Dad's gonna kill us. But what can you do?" He starts clapping his hands really hard. "Enjoy it, Brody! That's Arlo Guthrie a piss length away from us, singing a Bob Dylan song! Can you stand it?"

He's right. Forget about tomorrow. This is the coolest thing I've ever done in my life.

A while later I feel that Tang again. I've always had a small bladder. "Ryan, I gotta take a leak," I say.

He laughs and points up the hill. "Find yourself a tree with roots," he says.

I look up at the massive crowd and wonder how I'll ever find my way back to Ryan in the darkness. But there are small campfires on the hill, and the strobes from the stage are bright. I glance around for some landmarks—a guy in a sleeveless leather vest, a woman in a yellow sun hat—then trudge up the hill.

It takes several minutes to get clear of the crowd, and I just duck behind an overflowing trash barrel and piss. As I'm walking back I hear a familiar voice. "It's that kid," she says.

It's the two girls we picked up hitchhiking. I don't see the guys, but then again, I don't look around much. Not only aren't they wearing bras; they aren't wearing *anything* up top. First time I've seen the real thing in person. "Brady!" Annie says. She's wet with rain and spattered with mud.

"Brody," I say, my voice coming out all squeaky.

"Isn't this outasight?" She puts her hand on my shoulder, as if she's about to hug me. I think I'd pass out if she did.

The other one is hurrying across the hill and Annie yells, "Wait up," and follows, not even looking back at me or saying good-bye.

It takes a few minutes to find Ryan and Jenny and Skippy, but I feel pretty safe among all these peaceniks. When I reach them, they're sitting in a circle with a white guy with a big Afro and sunglasses and a huge woman with a red bandanna, and they're passing around a joint and a bottle of wine. Arlo Guthrie is singing "Amazing Grace," and there's a flash of lightning way in the distance. The rain is still steady.

I take off my shirt and make a little pillow and lie back in the soaking wet grass. Sooner or later I nod off.

SATURDAY, AUGUST 16:

What We're Made Of

Ryan nudges me awake just as Joan Baez is taking the stage wearing a greenish hippie dress with fringe and some kind of scarf and carrying an acoustic guitar. Jenny is jumping up and down and the crowd is roaring.

I couldn't have been asleep for more than fifteen minutes, but I feel wide awake immediately. I listen to Baez's folky protest music, but I mostly look around and can't believe there are this many people in one place who seem so different from everybody I've ever known. I mean, the war always seemed so far away until Ryan and Dad started fighting about it, and this whole idea of protesting and peacing out and standing up to the government just isn't the way it goes back home. You do what they say, right or wrong. Of course, an awful lot of these people are just here to get wasted. Skippy, for one, is lying facedown in the grass, partied out.

But I'm in the midst of more people than I've ever seen in one place, and none of them cares what their parents think right now or if anybody's staring at their breasts or whether a cop might come by and slap handcuffs on 'em for smoking weed. I can practically hear my dad: "Bunch of freeloading idiots. 'Peace and love, la-di-da.' Just wait till they have to get real jobs and haircuts. *That'll* be an amazing grace."

Ryan puts his arm around my shoulder and leans into my ear. "Things are changing right before our eyes," he says. He starts clapping his hands and whooping. "Stop the war!" he yells.

I yell, too. Anything to keep Ryan from going.

The concert ends for the night about the same time the rain does, sometime around three in the morning.

"We gotta haul ass," Ryan says. "We are so screwed when Dad gets ahold of us."

The good news—if you can call it that—is that nobody else is leaving the grounds at this hour, so we can make some time. There are people sleeping in heaps in the mud, but there are also lots of little tents pitched on the hill and other people rolled up in sleeping bags.

A guy with long stringy hair is handing out leaflets that say GET OUT OF 'NAM NOW, and we all take one. Ryan gives the guy a raised-fist salute and says, "Peace, brother."

We pass a pond and hear people splashing and laughing, and a naked guy and woman walk across the road right in front of us, saying, "Bath time!"

The dirt road is a total mud hole, but it gets better when we reach the highway.

I duck into the cemetery again to retrieve the cooler, and

they all follow me. "Thanks, Johnny," I say to the tombstone.

Ryan shines the flashlight on a gravestone just across from Townsend's. "Here's why what we did was right," he says. "Why you never pass up a chance for an experience like this."

The stone is simple:

LITTLE HARRY

Born April 27, 1884

Died May 21, 1884

"You never know when you'll take your last breath," Ryan says. "Grab your life and shake it."

It takes another two hours to reach the car, and we eat my mother's peanut butter sandwiches on the way. They're soggy from the rain, but we haven't eaten much since that pot roast.

The sun comes up, and there are patches of clear sky between the clouds.

There aren't a whole lot of abandoned cars behind us, so we're able to back the car up for about a quarter mile, then turn around and head for Port Jervis.

We pull into Aunt Lizzie's driveway a little before seven.

She's up, and the house smells like coffee and toast. Ryan calls home and luckily he gets Mom, who had called the New York State Police—twice—and was told about the impossibility of communication at the concert and that the Thruway was closed because of Woodstock traffic.

So me and Ryan and Skippy sit on the couch wearing fluffy pink towels around our naked bodies while Aunt

Lizzie washes our mud-soaked clothes. We watch *The Jetsons* and *Magilla Gorilla*, then eat homemade pancakes and fried eggs. Jenny falls asleep in an armchair, wearing nothing but a purple bathrobe. She's content; Joan Baez closed the show last night.

"I have a football game at one," I say, yawning for the hundredth time. We're more than an hour from home.

"No sweat," Ryan says. He looks happier than I've ever seen him. And that's saying something.

"Today we'll see what you're made of," Coach Epstein barks as we huddle up around him. "See how you handle yourselves against another team."

The players from Lodi are doing jumping jacks at the end of the field. This is a "controlled" scrimmage, not really a game, so we're still at the dirt practice field behind the high school and we're wearing our gray practice jerseys. Our real home games will be on Saturday nights under the lights at the athletic field next to the swim club. First one is only two weeks away.

Coach lowers his voice and looks around. "Don't let the chocolate ones scare you," he says. "They go down the same as anybody else when you hit 'em."

I look over at the Lodi players and see that they've got four black guys. We don't have any. There's not one black kid living in our town.

I try not to yawn but I can't help it.

"Am I boring you, Mr. Winslow?" Coach asks.

Some of the guys laugh.

"Sorry," I say, wiping my mouth. We got home in time for me to brush my teeth, eat a hamburger, and get into my uniform. No sleep except for maybe fifteen minutes in the grass last night.

"Discipline, boys," Coach says. "We're an army; that should be your mind-set."

It doesn't matter that I'm so tired, because I spend the entire afternoon kneeling on the sideline, watching. It's raining on and off, and the grassless field is a mess.

I know the coaches aren't happy that I skipped practice yesterday, but I did bring a written excuse from my mother today. After that run I made in practice the other day, I would think they'd give me some playing time.

Tony gets in at linebacker for a handful of plays, then he kneels next to me. His uniform is covered with mud like everybody else's—except for mine and Joey Salinardi's, that is.

Across the field, there are three or four Lodi players who haven't gotten in yet, either. We keep glancing at each other and sizing one another up. The scrimmage has been dead even.

Finally Coach Epstein waves me and Tony and Joey onto the field. It's our ball, and we huddle up around Coach. In a controlled scrimmage, the coaches stay on the field and call the plays.

Same formation as in practice: Joey at quarterback, Tony

at fullback, and me behind them at tailback. Coach calls that forty-six pitch and I feel a shiver. Salinardi catches my eye and whispers, "Break this one."

I glance at the defensive line, particularly the tackle and the end I'll be trying to cut between.

I immediately realize that I've made a dumb mistake, looking right at the hole I'll be heading for. Maybe they didn't notice.

Salinardi takes the snap, and I hesitate for a second before cutting right. The pitch is bad—low and almost behind me—but I should be able to grab it anyway. I don't.

The nose of the football hits me in the shin and falls straight down, then bounces away. I pivot and reach, but the defensive tackle is already on me, knocking me to the ground. I scramble to my feet, but a Lodi player scoops up the ball with a clear field ahead of him. I'm the only one with a shot at preventing a touchdown.

Not much of a shot. The guy is seven yards ahead of me in a full run. I chase him all the way to the end zone but never get any closer.

Coach Epstein blows his whistle. "That's all!" he yells. "Nice job by both teams."

So I got in for one stupid play and totally blew it.

"My fault," Salinardi says to me as we walk off the field. But nobody else will see it that way. I fumbled. I got knocked down. They scored. It's as simple as that, and it cost us the scrimmage.

At least I look like I played. I got as much mud on my uniform as if I'd played the whole time. Big deal.

"What happened?" Tony asks me as we run our laps.

"I don't know. The ball didn't get to me."

"It hit you."

"Wrong place."

"Still should have grabbed it. I bet we would have had ten more plays if we'd kept possession."

"You think?"

"Yeah. I would have carried on the next play. I guarantee it."

"Sorry."

Nobody else says anything to me, but there's nothing worse than costing your team a game. They worked all afternoon and kept things even, and then I got in for one play and wrecked the whole thing.

I bet the coaches are wishing they'd cut me when they had the chance.

"You walking home?" Tony asks.

We've walked home together after every practice. "How else would I get there? A helicopter?"

The cheerleaders showed up toward the end of the scrimmage, so guys like Esposito and Ferrante are hanging out by them, laughing and acting all cool.

I just want to get out of here. I'm exhausted.

And I'm the worst player on this team.

SUNDAY, AUGUST 17

Woodstock Flock

By Brody Winslow

Marching
Not to battle
Marching
All night long
Marching
Past barns and cattle
Marching
To hear a song

Marching
With my brother
Marching
With thousands more
Marching
To hear another
Marching
Against the war

Playing It Smooth

There's a long line at the water fountain after practice, so me and Tony just head up to Fisher's for soda. The coaches set up our kicking teams today, since the opening game is coming up. They put me at end on the kickoff squad because I'm fast and elusive.

My job is to sprint straight down the field and then do a box-and-in, making a hard right turn when I reach the twenty-yard line, cutting off the sideline.

They cut the laps down to two and we do only three wind sprints, but we're all soaked with sweat and dying of thirst by the end anyway.

We run into Janet and Patty, the girls from the swim club.

Well, we don't exactly run into them. They're sitting at Fisher's counter drinking milk shakes. I go to the cooler for bottles of soda. Tony walks over to the girls and sets his helmet on the stool next to Patty. I'd rather just ignore them, and I'm sure they'd prefer that, too.

"Nice and cool in here," Tony says. "Man, it was brutal out there in the sun, knocking people down all afternoon."

Patty gives half a nod and keeps looking at her milk shake. Janet swivels on her stool so she's partly facing Tony. She smiles a lot more often than Patty. "Swim club's staying open late tonight," she says. "Night swim."

"That's good," Tony says. "We'll be there."

"Us, too."

The swim club usually closes at seven, but when it's this hot they sometimes stretch it to nine or even ten.

"I'm just gonna lie on the bottom of the pool for like ten minutes and cool off," Tony says.

Patty frowns. "Sure."

"I got great lungs," he says. He picks up his helmet. "So, we'll see you there. I just gotta stop home and eat and shave, maybe have a beer or two. See ya."

Janet says, "See ya." Patty doesn't.

Tony's trying to make himself look taller as he pays for his soda. He doesn't look back as we leave the store, but as soon as we hit the sidewalk he goes, "Man, this is gonna be great."

"What is?"

"Tonight, stupid. Didn't you hear them?"

I just look at him. He swings his helmet at me and hits my shoulder pads. "Night swim? They're wondering if we're gonna be there? What are you, blind?"

"What are you talking about?"

He rolls his eyes and shakes his head. "Just follow my

lead, okay?" He juts his thumb back in the direction we came. "They want us, Brody. You couldn't see that?"

All I could see was Patty acting like she wished Tony would go away. And I can't imagine anybody "wanting" us with our scrawny bodies and clueless personalities. I mean, I couldn't act cool even if I wanted to—I don't know how. I've tried in front of the mirror.

Janet only mentioned the night swim because Tony said how hot he was.

But I'll go along. A night swim is a good excuse to get out of the house for the evening. Why spoil it by pursuing two girls who'd rather we keep our distance?

Ryan's at Shop-Rite and Dad's working late, so Mom fries me up a hamburger and some leftover potatoes. She says it's no problem if I go swimming with Tony tonight.

I read a *Mad* magazine while I eat, but then I pick up the *Herald-News*. I usually only read the sports and the comics, but tonight I scan the front page for the heck of it. Two big battles yesterday in Da Nang; lots of soldiers killed. The second-strongest hurricane ever recorded is hitting the southern states. The Mets are on the front page, too, for a change. They swept two straight doubleheaders from the Padres the past couple of days.

Tony comes by around seven fifteen. "How was the beer?" I ask, knowing full well that he didn't have any. He doesn't have to shave yet, either.

"I just said that for them."

"No kidding. I'm sure they were real impressed by your maturity."

My dad keeps a case of Rheingold in the old refrigerator in the cellar, so I have tried beer. It's rancid, bitter stuff.

"Still hot," Tony says, wiping his face with his hand as we walk down the hill. Most of the town is way higher than the area where the swim club and the football field are. Route 17 is on the other side of those things, and from there the land is basically flat across Teterboro and all the way to the Hudson River and the city.

The swim club is crowded: men home from work and families and a lot of teenagers. We throw our shirts and sneakers in the locker room and walk around the perimeter of the grounds, staying on the grass. The entire swim club is about the size of two football fields side by side, with a cement apron around the edge of the pool.

The pool is shaped like a T—twenty-five meters long, with diving boards at the far end. There are fifteen-meter wings off the shallower end and a kiddie pool over to the side. (I know the measurements because I was on the swim team the past three summers, specializing in the breaststroke. I didn't go out this year because of football.)

We've got a blacktop basketball court over by the locker rooms and a big grass area behind the pool, fenced off from the highway. Janet and Patty are lying on their towels in the grass with a couple of older girls. Janet sees us coming and nudges Patty. Patty looks up quickly, then turns her head the other way, staying flat.

Tony's leading the way. He walks past, about ten feet from them, pretending he doesn't see them. "Let's go shoot some hoops," he says to me, loud enough so they can hear.

So we check out a basketball from the office. The court is empty, and it's no secret why. The blacktop is about a thousand degrees.

"No way I'm going barefoot on that," I say. So we go to the locker room and put our sneakers back on. There's a poster on the wall I didn't notice before.

END-OF-SUMMER SWIM CLUB DANCE
Ages 13 to 18
Thursday, August 28
Music by The Electrons
8–10:30 p.m.
Free for Members. $1.50 Guests

Tony reads the poster slowly. "How would they know how old we are?" he asks.

"Our birth dates are on our membership cards."

"They won't check every card."

"Maybe not." But people know how old we are, whether it's on the card or not. Like we could walk into a dance that's mostly for high school kids and nobody would notice! We'd get thrown out on our butts.

We play three games of O-U-T (I win twice) then ditch the basketball and head for the water.

There are more people in the water than out, which is unusual, but the temperature is still over ninety degrees. They've closed off the diving boards so more people can swim in that area. We swim underwater across the shallow end and come up on the other side of the ropes.

Tony spits out a huge stream of water and strokes over to the edge to get a look at Patty and Janet.

"They see you?" I ask.

"They've been looking right at us. They looked away when I caught them staring."

He's dreaming. They're in the group that has parties on the weekends and clusters together on the Boulevard after school. The ones in that group are our age, but the guys have muscles and attitudes. "They hang out with Stephie and Esposito and those people," I say.

"Not always. Besides, we could hang with that group if we wanted to."

No way. "Once you're in that group, you're in, and nobody else can penetrate."

"Things change in the summer," Tony says. "Besides, here they come."

We hang on the wall and watch as they slowly walk all the way around to the far steps, tucking their hair under their racing caps as they go. Janet is in the same green two-piece she always wears, but Patty has a skimpier pinkish one I haven't seen before, and she keeps pulling it down where it's creeping up her cheeks.

I keep staring until they dive in.

They glide out toward the middle of the pool and I lose sight of them behind some adults. But I keep watching, and eventually Patty comes into view and looks right at us. She ducks under the water and comes up ten feet farther away, back turned.

"Oh yeah, they're *real* interested," I say.

Tony slaps at the water and it splashes into my face. "Don't you know anything about how girls work?" he asks. "They don't throw themselves at you." He lowers his voice. "Just keep playing it smooth, like I am."

"Real smooth," I say.

"Shut up. I know what I'm doing." He starts swimming toward them, underwater. I stay back.

When he pops up, I see Janet laugh. He spits water at her this time, and she splashes him back. Patty starts swimming toward the diving area.

She swims right past me, as if she's working out, but she turns her head and says, "Hi." No emotion behind it or anything. Just "Hi."

"Hi," I say, but it perks up my interest. She had no reason to say anything to me. So when she stops at the end of the pool and treads water, I call over to her. "Feels good, huh?"

She brightens just slightly and says, "Yep," but she doesn't look at me. She starts waving at Janet, who's still with Tony, smiling and talking. "I'm getting out!" she yells.

She climbs out right there and a whistle blows. You're supposed to use the ladders or the steps. She looks over to the lifeguard station and frowns. The guard, who is almost directly above me, says, "You know better."

Patty lifts her shoulders and looks up at the guard, saying, "Sorry," all insincere. But then she looks down at me and gives the faintest hint of a smile before walking away.

Tony swims over to me about thirty seconds later. "You better practice dancing when you get home tonight, bro."

"Why?"

"We're taking them to that thing next week."

"What thing?"

"The dance."

"Get out."

"I ain't kidding. I mean, we're not exactly taking them, but I convinced Janet to get Patty to sneak in. So we'll be the only twelve-year-olds there. Who else are they gonna hang out with, right?"

I look over toward Patty, but I can't see her. She must be lying down. Tony must figure he'll be with her, but it's pretty obvious she can't stand him.

She said "Hi" to me though. Even said "Yep" about the water feeling good.

What's there to dancing anyway? You just move your arms up and down. I saw lots of that at Woodstock.

I can handle it. I think.

Bottom of the Fourteenth

S o the Mets have won four straight, but I'm not getting caught up in that anymore. They just let you down. The Padres are even worse than they are, so beating them four times isn't saying much.

We got chewed out by my father pretty good this weekend for staying out all night at the Woodstock concert, but even he had to admit we had no choice.

"Of course, you could have chosen not to go," he said. "But that would have taken some common sense, which you two seem to lack rather badly."

Hey, Dad, I was just along for the ride. And you told us it was okay. It was Mom who was against it.

So I lie on my bed and listen to WMCA all evening. They play "Honky Tonk Women" every thirty-seven seconds.

I'm not looking forward to summer ending. I've spent seven years at Euclid School around the corner; now I'll have to walk another six blocks to Franklin. That school's just for the seventh and eighth grades, so we'll be the little kids again. Plus we'll be joining up with the kids who went to Lincoln Elementary. I know a few of them from football and the swim club, and they seem weird and dumber than the people on this side of town.

I doze off and probably sleep for an hour before Ryan opens my door and turns the light on. "Spinning Wheel" is just ending, and Ryan says, "Switch to the Mets. You won't believe this game!"

So I turn the dial and hear Ralph Kiner saying, "Top of the fourteenth."

"Fourteenth *inning*?" I say.

"Yeah. And it's scoreless," Ryan says. "Marichal has pitched every inning for the Giants."

"Who's in for the Mets?"

"McGraw. Gentry pitched the first ten."

I've never heard of such a thing. Thirteen innings without any runs? When I played Little League, people were scoring constantly.

Ryan sits on the floor with his back against the wall, knees up. "The Mets are totally happening all of a sudden."

I shrug. They've flattened my enthusiasm too many times before. "Dad stop yelling at you?" I ask.

He waves his hand sort of disgustedly. "He never really yelled. Just acted like I'm stupid and irresponsible."

"Acted?" I remember Dad saying those things pretty directly.

He strokes his chin, where the soft, thin hairs are about a half-inch long and curling under, and lets out a sigh. We listen to the game for a couple of minutes before he speaks again. "Big changes coming, Brody."

"A pinch hitter?"

He laughs. "In the world." He takes a sheet of paper out of his pocket; it's the flyer we picked up at the concert. "We've had it with this war, the establishment—everything. Woodstock was just the start."

"What can you do about it?"

"Stick it to 'em," he says. "Protest."

Dad pushes the door open; Ryan didn't shut it tight like I always do. He steps into the room but doesn't say anything.

Ryan ignores him. "Our brothers are dying over there, Brody. Forty thousand dead, and Nixon would double that if he had his way."

Dad clears his throat. He and Ryan look at each other, not exactly glaring, but not too friendly, either.

"Ryan," Dad says, "you are so full of crap it's coming out your ears."

"It's an unjust war, Dad."

"It's *our* war," he says sharply.

Ryan shakes his head and looks at the ceiling.

McGraw has retired the Giants, so it's still scoreless going into the bottom of the fourteenth.

Dad picks up a stack of baseball cards from my dresser and looks at the top one. "It'll be *your* war if you don't smarten up," he says.

61

Ryan will turn eighteen on September 9. Mom's been worried sick. He'll be eligible for the draft.

"You didn't go," Ryan says, staring at the radio.

"I'm forty-two years old, bub."

"You know what I mean."

Dad got excused from military service. Asthma or something like that; the heart trouble came later. He sets down the cards and stares at Ryan. "College students get deferments."

"I'll go to Canada."

"Oh yeah, that's a great answer. Freeze your nuts off in an igloo when you could be getting an education."

We went to Canada a couple of summers ago for the World's Fair: Expo 67 in Montreal. It wasn't cold at all. Then again, it was the middle of the summer. We pitched a tent in a giant field in the city with a thousand other tents and trailers. Everything was wet and the entire area smelled from the portable toilets.

"The war is immoral," Ryan says.

"You're so full of—"

"You said that already."

"Yeah, well you never listen anyway." Dad sits on the edge of my bed and looks at the radio. The Mets already have one out, but Agee is up. Marichal is *still* pitching.

Dad turns to me. "So what's your excuse, Lucifire?"

"For what?"

"For living." He's joking around now. That's his way—cut into Ryan, then try to take the pressure off through me.

I start to speak, but the radio catches our attention. "Well hit and deep. This could be—that ball is gone! Tommie Agee with a walk-off homer in the bottom of the fourteenth, and the Mets win their fifth in a row!"

"Amazing!" Dad says, standing up.

Ryan raises a fist. "Freaking out!"

"Who are these guys?" Dad says, grinning broadly. "It can't be our Mets." He holds out one palm and Ryan slaps it, then Ryan holds out his own palm for Dad.

"We gotta get to a game," Ryan says. "No more talking about it. We gotta go."

"Well . . . we'll see," Dad says. "Where's a schedule?"

I go over to my dresser and take a schedule out of the top drawer. "They got a few more home games, then a long road trip," I say. "They'll be in California until September."

Dad slowly rolls his head from side to side. "Brody will be in school by then," he says. "But there's always the radio and TV."

"Can't we say *maybe* in September we'll go?" Ryan says.

"Maybe. But not likely."

"Of course, by then they might lose ten in a row," I say.

Dad laughs. "I got a good feeling this season, buddy. Agee, Seaver, Koosman—these guys are the real thing." He raises his voice and it gets kind of squeaky. "That ball is *gone!*"

He leaves a few seconds later—whistling "Meet the Mets"—and Ryan pushes the door shut. He looks at me and shakes his head, but he's smiling. "What was that all about?" he whispers.

"I don't know." But I kind of do. Dad's been riding Ryan

hard all summer, but I know it's because he's worried about him. Every morning on the radio we hear about the bomb- ings and the invasions while Dad eats his stale pound cake for breakfast. We all know the days before Ryan's birthday are ticking like a time bomb. He hasn't done anything about applying to college.

We listen to the post-game, then I switch back to music. We catch the end of Stevie Wonder, then they play "Honky Tonk Women" *again*.

"I'm getting a little tired of that one," I say as it ends. Ryan gives a half smile and nods. He hasn't said anything for a while, just sitting there. I don't envy him.

The Youngbloods come on. My favorite song this week.

> *Come on people now*
>
> *Smile on your brother*
>
> *Everybody get together*
>
> *Try to love one another right now*

Vietnam. He could be there by Halloween.

Hell, he could be dead by then.

He wouldn't be the first.

And we all know it.

WEDNESDAY, AUGUST 20:

Straight at Me

Ferrante's calling signals as he looks over the helmets of the linemen, directly at me: the middle linebacker.

Peter Sarnoski limped off the field a second ago, and Coach Epstein pointed to the first guy he saw on the sideline to take his place. It happened to be me.

Ferrante slings a short pass over the middle, right toward me. The tight end is coming my way and he steps in front of me and catches the ball. I wrap my arms around his legs and another linebacker helps me finish the job.

They'll be working on me, that's for sure—thinking I'm the weak spot. I brush some dirt off my thigh.

I glance at the sideline. There are three or four people kneeling there who probably should be in here instead. Tough luck. I got it.

Ferrante's no dope. He calls that same pass route from the opposite side, and I see it coming but don't have time to react. Eddie Lorenzo grabs the pass and tries to stiff-arm me, but I duck under and get hold of his leg. He drags me a few yards, but he goes down.

I've made two tackles in two plays, but we're backing up fast.

Coach calls time and huddles up the defenders. "This is where tough guys toughen up!" he growls. "First and goal, backs to the wall. Let's see what you've got."

Coach grabs my face mask and glares at me. Then he turns to Finken, who's at middle guard. "They're coming right at you two, and you know it!" he says. "Smashmouth football, right up the gut. Let's stop 'em cold!"

"Readeeeeee," Ferrante calls, hunched over the line. "Ready, set . . . hut, hut." He takes the snap and cradles the ball, lunging behind the center as Finken is shoved aside. I step into the gap and meet Ferrante head-on, standing him up just long enough for help to arrive and stop him for no gain.

"They're coming at you again, middle men," Coach says. "What kind of candy are you made of?"

I let out my breath hard. This isn't so bad. It's like playing in the lot up on Roosevelt Avenue. Only difference is the matching uniforms and the coaches.

Come at me again. I'm ready.

Ferrante drops back. Lorenzo's in my face, reaching for the pass, but I duck under his shoulder and deflect the ball to the ground.

My hand stings. I shake it. Lorenzo yells, "Pass interference," but Coach waves him off and says, "Get back to the huddle, pansy."

These guys are big and quick and have a lot more experience than I do. They're busting my chops on every play, expecting me to fail.

Keep coming at me.

Same play again? Lorenzo is running toward me like a freight train. I pivot, timing my hit so I'll get there just as the ball does.

But there's no pass. Lorenzo comes up from under me with a brutal block. I see stars as his forearm meets my mouth, and I fall backward to the dirt.

I lie there for a few seconds, in the end zone. Esposito is standing over me with the ball. He scored.

Coach pushes Esposito aside and looks down at me. "You all right?" he asks.

I sit up and spit out my mouth guard. I reach for my jaw and it feels okay, so I nod. But my fingers are bloody when I take them away. I can taste the blood, too, but just on the outside of my lip. No big deal.

"Better sit out until that stops bleeding," Coach says. "Offense's ball at the twenty, going the other way."

Sarnoski comes back onto the field, so that'll be the end of it for me. I join Tony and the other subs on the sideline.

Nobody says anything about my performance, but I'm feeling good about it as we leave the field after practice. They came at me on every play and I held my own. I stuck 'em right back.

My lip is stinging and I can feel it starting to swell, so I check it in the side mirror of Coach's Wonder Bread truck as we pass through the parking lot.

There's a crust of dried blood and dirt covering about a third of my lower lip. No way I'm wiping that off.

"Lucky break today," Tony says. "Getting in there with the first string."

I shrug. Lucky or not, I made the most of it.

"How's your face feel?"

"Feels all right," I say. "Looks good, too."

"Looks awesome."

We reach the Boulevard and turn right. It's a twelve-block walk home (two more for Tony), but I don't mind. I like being seen in my football stuff. Football is big here; we're one of the few towns in the county with a lighted field for Friday night high school games. Most of the other high school teams play on Saturday afternoons, and the junior football teams play on Sundays. We go Saturday nights for our home games, and the crowds are big. Not like Friday nights, of course, but big enough.

Tony grabs my wrist as we're approaching Corpus Christi. "Look over there," he says, jutting his chin toward the other side of the street. Janet and Patty are sitting on the steps of the church.

"Let's cross," he says.

"You really want to keep bugging them?" I ask.

He frowns and gives me a light shove. "Who's bugging who?" he asks. "You think they don't know when practice is over? That we walk past here every day at a quarter to six?"

Maybe he's onto something. I touch my lip, feeling the crust. I swing my helmet at him and we cross the street.

"Ladies," Tony says.

Janet turns her head as if she's looking for the ladies he might be referring to. But she looks back and says, "Men."

Tony puts his foot on the bottom step, in front of Patty. I glance up at the church, which is huge and mysterious and kind of freaks me out. Seems like everybody I know goes here except us. I mean, there are at least six Protestant churches in town, too, but all together, I think the Catholics way outnumber us Methodists and Lutherans and Presbyterians. The guys I know who go here are scared to death of the priests.

"Looks like you got beat up," Janet says to me.

Tony waves her off. "You should see the other guy. We hammered 'em good today. Blood all over the place."

"You got some on your shirt," Patty says, finally speaking.

I look down. There's a small streak of blood above the 3. (My practice number is 43; I don't know what my game jersey number will be yet.)

"I'll survive," I say. And I don't know why, but I take a seat next to Patty, not close or anything, but on the same step. I stretch out my legs and look at the traffic.

"So what are you girls doing here?" Tony asks. "You have catechism class or something?"

"No," Janet replies. "Just killing time."

"We got school in two weeks," Tony says. "Less than that, even. Where'd the summer go?"

Patty yawns. "Two weeks is a long time."

"You going to Franklin?" Tony asks.

Patty shakes her head slowly. "We'll still be here." She nods back toward the church.

Corpus Christi goes from first grade through eighth, but I know a lot of kids who've gone back and forth from there to the public schools. They say the nuns are nasty teachers. Who knows if that's true. I've had some nasty teachers at Euclid, too, but mostly not.

We sit there for about five minutes, talking about nothing. I used to have friends who were girls back when I was little, but things shifted a lot the past couple of years. By fourth grade you got ragged on just for talking to one, but in fifth some couples started pairing up. By sixth grade you either had a girlfriend or you didn't, and everybody knew who didn't.

So this feels different, sitting here, watching cars go by and listening to Tony yammering about music and television shows. Janet definitely seems to like him, laughing at things he says that are really lame. Patty keeps looking out at the street like there's something interesting going on out there.

I figure there must be, too. I just don't know what it is yet.

THURSDAY, AUGUST 21:

Kind of Poetic

They had another night swim tonight, but there was no sign of Patty and Janet.

"They can't make it too obvious," Tony says as we're walking up the hill. "Believe me, they know what they're doing."

The sun is down, but there's still a bit of light. I'm dragging my butt, worn out from another hard practice. It cooled off about a quarter degree, so the coaches had us running lots of laps and sprints.

My hair is dripping; we were the last ones out of the pool at nine, and the lifeguards hustled us through the gate in a hurry.

As we get near my house, we see Ryan and my father in the driveway. My dad is yelling at Ryan, but not loud enough that we can hear him. He yells in a way that doesn't carry, but it pierces.

I look at Tony.

"Guess I'll see ya tomorrow," he says.

"Right." I hesitate for a few seconds, then head up our sidewalk.

"Do you have any idea how hot it gets in that car during the day?" Dad is saying. "It's been in the nineties all week; it's probably been a hundred and forty in the car."

"Mom made us take it."

"She didn't make you leave it in my backseat for the hottest week of the year!"

I swallow hard. Did those hitchhikers leave pot in the car?

The back hatch is open. Ryan reaches in and grimaces as he lifts out a dripping chunk of green and brown goop.

The watermelon.

"It's bad enough you put your little brother in jeopardy with that all-night stunt at the hippie circus," Dad says. "But you stink my car up to high heaven with a rotten corpse."

"I haven't even been in the car since we got back."

"Oh, hell's bells, Ryan. You're the one who left the stupid melon in there."

Ryan keeps pulling bits of the melon out of the back and tossing them over the hedges that line the driveway.

"You'll need to scrub that floor clean," Dad says.

Ryan frowns and nods. "I will."

"Keep the hatch open all day tomorrow so the sun can shine on that spot," Dad says. "Make sure it doesn't rain."

"No problem."

Dad goes in the house. Ryan flicks a bit of rotten melon at me and smiles.

I duck out of the way. "That's gross."

We take a seat on the curb. Ryan starts laughing. "Dad drove down to the hardware store after dinner. He said he's driving around wondering what smells so bad. So he rolls up the windows because he figures it must be outside. It got so bad in the car he almost puked."

I turn and look at the station wagon. Even from eight feet away I can smell it. "It *is* pretty bad."

"It's disgusting. But nobody's even moved the car since we got back."

Mom walks to the swim club every day, and she does the food shopping on Friday mornings. Dad got his beer for the week on Saturday afternoon when the melon was still intact. So the thing had the better part of a week to go bad in there without anybody noticing.

Dad comes out of the house with a bucket of soapy water and a brush. He's also got two cans of Rheingold and one of Shop-Rite lemon soda cradled against his chest. He puts the bucket next to the car and hands me the soda. He nods to Ryan and sets a beer on the hood of the car, then pops open his own and takes a long swig.

Ryan starts scrubbing. Dad sits on the curb next to me with a giant grin. He holds up his beer and says, "Cheers, LaZe-kiel."

"You got an opener?" I ask. The beers have pop-tops, but the soda doesn't.

He nods and reaches into the pocket of his shorts for the opener. "Put some elbow grease into that," he says to Ryan, but his voice is way different now, like he's joking around.

"Nothing like the smell of rotten melon on a summer evening," Ryan says. "It's kind of poetic, you know? The moon, the crickets, the unbelievably nauseating aroma."

"It's one of the true natural wonders," Dad says, going along with the new direction of the conversation. He stands and steps over to the car, inspecting Ryan's work.

"Dump that in the gutter," Dad says, pointing to the bucket. "Sit down and take a load off."

Ryan dumps the suds, and the water rushes down the hill. "That one mine?" he asks, pointing to the beer on the hood.

"If you want it."

"I do."

So we sit on the curb, our legs stretched out into the street, and look up at the stars. Dad points out constellations.

"There's Orion," he says. "And the Big Dipper, of course." He motions toward the horizon with his beer. "That one's Brody, the horse's ass. And over there"—he points above the neighbor's house—"that's Ryan, the wandering knuckle-head."

"Anybody know how the Mets did?" Ryan asks.

"They were losing the last I checked," Dad replies. "They've won six straight, though."

"Don't blink," I say. "Before you know it they'll *lose* six in a row."

Dad leans back and winks at Ryan. "How'd your little brother turn into such a pessimist?" he asks.

"Beats me," Ryan says. "Come on, Brody. You gotta believe. This is their season. I'm feeling it."

A car goes by, way too fast for this street, and we pull our legs in. "Slow down, Henry!" Dad says. He calls every bad driver Henry. I don't know if that's out of the Bible or what. Maybe he saves all the biblical names for me.

Ryan takes a swig of his beer. "I don't want to kill people," he says softly, jumping into that conversation they've been having all summer. It's always there, even if a week goes by without any real talking. "I sure as hell don't want to be *forced* to kill people."

Dad hesitates and looks down the hill. "You have an option," he says.

"Yeah," Ryan says softly, "but that's being forced on me, too. I'm not ready for college. Cowards avoid conflict. I'm not avoiding anything."

Dad shakes his head slowly. "Well, I guess you're trying to make sense. . . . Not quite succeeding, though."

We're quiet until the cans are empty. The crickets are even louder now. The night feels cooler for a change, but the mosquitoes are swarming anyway.

"It'd be different if the war was here," Ryan says. "If they were trying to kill Mom or Brody or Jenny. I'd be first in line then. But I ain't about to get ambushed over in that swamp . . . get a bayonet stabbed between my ribs. Why the hell are we even over there?"

Dad scrunches up his face in a frown. "It's complicated," he says.

"It's bullshit."

We sit there for another ten minutes or so until Dad stands up and yawns. He holds out a hand and pulls Ryan to his feet. They look at each other for a few seconds, not glaring this time, just looking.

I get up on my own and head inside to see if I can catch the end of the Mets game.

FRIDAY, AUGUST 22:

Plenty of Grease

After *The Price Is Right*, Mom asks if I want to go to the swim club with her.

"I don't know," I say, switching off the television. "I might go down later with Tony."

I feel a little sorry for Mom. I was four when the swim club opened, so she and I went every day. She'd sit under a big umbrella with other ladies and watch their kids splash in the kiddie pool, then she'd take me into the big pool and teach me to swim. For the next few summers we were there all the time, but then I started spending more time with Tony. She's still there every day, but I hardly ever go with her.

"You sure are having a busy summer," she says. "Want lunch?"

"Yeah."

I sit on Dad's high stool at the counter while she fries up some ham for my sandwich. "Big scrimmage tomorrow," I say, "so I figure I ought to rest up."

She gives me a small smile and says, "Mmm-hmm."

"But maybe I will go with you. Just lie on a towel and get some sun."

"That would be nice," she says. "I'd like the company."

I pick up a saltshaker and turn it around in my hand. It's a tall, clear one, with a few grains of rice mixed in with the salt. I always wondered about that. "Why is there rice in here?" I ask.

"It absorbs moisture. Keeps the salt from clumping up."

"Oh." The salt is clumpy anyway.

I exhale. "What, umm . . . You think Ryan . . ."

"I think he'd better do something soon," she says. "That application to Drew has been sitting on his desk all summer. So far he filled out the line that asks for his name. You want toast?"

"Yeah."

"Get it. This is almost ready."

I put two slices of bread in the toaster and wait. When it pops up, she grabs it and sticks the ham between the slices.

I take a big mouthful.

"This is no game," she says. "Kids like him are the first ones they send to the front lines. It could be too late already; his birthday's in two weeks."

I swallow. The ham sticks in my throat. "Ryan says the war is immoral."

"I voted for Nixon because he said he'd get us out, but he just keeps digging in deeper."

The phone rings and she goes to the hall to answer it. I can hear her talking about some library board issues.

When she comes back she asks if I'd like her to fry more ham. "There's plenty of grease."

I think about it. "Sure." I could stand to gain a few pounds.

She puts another slice of butter in the pan. "*I'll* drive him to Canada if it comes to that," she says. "They're not taking my child. Not for this war. Not for some pointless intervention."

I lie facedown in the grass near my mother's umbrella, the sun beating down on my back, and think about football and that dance next week and Ryan's situation.

The grass smells grassy. Patches of it are very dry, but here by the kiddie pool, there are a lot of dripping children, so it stays well watered.

I feel a splash of warm water on my back and look up. It's Tony, wiping his mouth.

"I banged on your door for ten minutes," he says. "You were supposed to wait for me."

I push up onto my elbow. "I guess I forgot."

"Jerk. . . . Hi, Mrs. Winslow."

"Hi, Tony."

I stand up and we walk toward the locker room. "They here?" I ask.

"I don't think so. They're not usually around this early."

"Right." I don't know what we'd do if those girls were here. Walk past and pretend we don't notice them again?

Every day's been like this all summer. Get up way too early with my dad, watch TV all morning after he leaves, have lunch and hit the pool with Tony, go to practice. Maybe school won't be so bad after all. Lots of possibilities.

Tomorrow's scrimmage is an intrasquad, but we'll be on the big field. They even hired a couple of referees, so it'll be run like a game, with the clock and the scoreboard and everything. They're handing out the game jerseys tonight after practice, but I'm on the side that'll wear the practice grays. With the team split in two, I ought to get a good bit of playing time on both offense and defense.

We wander around for an hour, shoot some baskets, then go home.

Yeah, it was boring, but that's life. Boring isn't always so bad.

SATURDAY, AUGUST 23:

A Scared Rabbit

The game jersey is dark blue with an orange number 27 and stripes on the sleeves. Looks a little strange. I'll be wearing the gray practice top for the scrimmage. Our pants are solid white and our helmets are solid blue; we wear the same ones for practices and games.

What's weird is the game socks. They're bright orange like the numbers and the sleeve stripes. Kind of Halloweeny. I was hoping for blue.

We're kicking off. Most of the top players are on the other team—Ferrante, Esposito, Magrini—but we have some good people, too. Tony is with my team, at the opposite end of the kickoff squad.

We're finally getting the remnants of that hurricane that hit the Gulf—just a strong breeze and some on-and-off rain. The grass—what a concept, playing football on grass after three weeks on dirt—is wet but doesn't seem too slippery.

Esposito is down near the goal line, waiting to return the kick. I'm not looking forward to colliding with him at full speed.

The referee blows his whistle. I take a quick glance at the bleachers. There are maybe a hundred people watching; my parents are up there.

The cheerleaders are on the cinder track. Guess they have to cheer for both teams.

The kick is high and kind of short. I watch it for a second before coming to my senses and darting down the field.

Box-and-in. Box-and-in. Esposito has the ball and is already past the twenty, coming straight up the middle. So I box in at the thirty-five. By luck I time it just right, because he jukes past a tackler and cuts toward me, angling past two others but slowing down as he searches for an opening.

I dive at his legs and wrap my arms around him. He shakes me loose, but I've stopped his progress and two of my teammates take him down.

Feels great to make that first hit. I jump up. Mitchell is on top of Esposito. He gets up and yells, "Yes!" smacking my hand.

We trot off the field. Coach Epstein says, "Nice hustle."

I walk to the bench and hold a paper cup under the watercooler, then take a drink. The cheerleaders are waving their pom-poms and yelling, "Go, Bulldogs!"

For today, my side is the Bulls and the other is the Dogs. I step to the sideline to watch, next to Tony.

It doesn't take long for the Dogs to score.

"Return team!" calls Coach Powell, who's in charge of our side today.

So I'm back on the field. I'm not usually on the return squad, but for this scrimmage I am. Me and Tony are midway back, on opposite sides.

The kick is way short. It bounces between us and we run toward it. Tony scoops it up and collides with me, then turns upfield and is swamped by tacklers. The ball comes loose and Magrini falls on it.

"Nice going," Tony says to me as we jog off the field.

"What?" He was the one who fumbled.

"You knocked the ball out of my hands."

"No, I didn't."

"Yeah, you did."

By halftime it's 33–0, so Coach Epstein makes Ferrante and Salinardi switch teams (and jerseys).

Aside from the kickoffs—and there have been a lot of them—neither me nor Tony has seen any action.

Technically we're the third-string running backs, but I can guarantee that even if Esposito, Delcalzo, Mitchell, and Colaneri went down with injuries, the coaches would shuffle things around so we'd still be substitutes. They'd put Stephie Jungerman in before I ever started at tailback.

Coach Powell finally sends us in for the start of the fourth quarter.

Ferrante looks at me, then at Tony, then back at me. "Let's try the forty-five pitch," he says. "On one."

I line up behind Tony, hands on my knees, and try to resist looking at the space between the left tackle and end. I've never run this play to the left. Since it's a pitchout, I'll have to catch it on my weaker side.

The gap is big and I dart through it. Tony slows a linebacker and I head toward the sideline, running like a scared rabbit. Esposito takes me down, but I gain at least six yards.

Tony leaps and punches me in the shoulder. "Way to move!" he says.

Tony gains about half a yard on the next play, and Ferrante seems hesitant in the huddle as we regroup. "Forty-six pitch," he says slowly. "No, wait. . . . Okay, forty-six pitch. On two."

That's Magrini's side of the field, and he's been making tackles for losses all afternoon. Ferrante steps back and waves us closer. "Hit the line fast," he whispers to Tony. "I'll be behind you." He shifts his eyes to me. "Follow me."

Tony runs through the line and makes contact with the middle linebacker. I fake to the right and shift back as the secondary converges on us, taking two steps past the line and diving.

They pile up on me, but I'm sure I have the first down, just short of midfield. The referee signals that I do.

Ferrante claps his hands hard in the huddle. "We're moving," he says. "We're marching."

But Tony gets only a yard on first down, and I can get only one more on second. Ferrante throws a long incompletion on third down and then gets sacked on fourth.

Esposito goes forty-two yards for a touchdown a few plays later, and suddenly it's 40–0.

"That sure turned in a hurry," Tony says, shaking his head.

"We were in a groove," I say. "We'll get it back."

The score is meaningless. We need a drive. We keep it on the ground and start eating up yardage again: Tony for three, me for four. It's basic stuff, handoffs up the middle.

We cross midfield. Ferrante calls the pitchout again. I can see myself making a couple of moves, outrunning the secondary, and reaching the end zone. I can taste it.

I take the pitch and dart past Lorenzo, but he sticks out a hand and pulls my arm back, causing me to bobble the ball. I duck to my right and hold on, but I'm forced to spin hard to regain my footing, and I get blindsided by a linebacker. The ball comes loose. I can't find it. Neither can my teammates. Lorenzo dives on it and yells, "Mine!"

"You gotta hold on to that ball!" Coach Powell says as I reach the sideline. "Fumbles kill football teams. They cost us games!"

I stand by myself, keeping my helmet on so no one can see my eyes, and watch the minutes tick away on the clock. Salinardi leads a methodical drive down the field, and the game ends with them at the fifteen-yard line.

We were moving the ball. And just like last week, I fumbled it away.

No way I'll ever carry it again. No way I'll get another chance.

SUNDAY, AUGUST 24

Pains
By Brody Winslow

Fumble-itis
Is like appendicitis
It gets inside us
And hurts

Four Years of Basket-Weaving

I sat around for the rest of the weekend and listened to the radio. Tony stopped by on Sunday, but I didn't leave the house. No motivation.

I just went through the motions at practice today, but nobody noticed. The coaches spent most of the time installing new plays—an end around reverse, a screen pass. I sat and watched. Maybe I should quit before the games start.

If there's any good news, it's that the Mets have won nine out of ten. But there isn't any good news as far as I'm concerned. Not after that fumble on Saturday.

I woke up at three in the morning that night, sweating after dreaming that I was carrying a watermelon across the Sea of Tranquility, running as fast as I could as the rain poured down and lightning struck. I dropped the melon and kicked it as I tried to pick it up, and it rolled down a grassy hill faster than I could ever run in my life. When I turned back I was naked and sixty thousand people in football uniforms were calling me Sue and yelling at me to get off the football field. Forever.

Then the people in football uniforms turned into Vietcong, and I watched helplessly as Ryan got gunned down, right in front of the stage and Arlo Guthrie.

Sounds funny, huh? Try dreaming it. It isn't.

Here's my new top five songs:

- "Get Together" (The Youngbloods)
- "Jean" (Oliver)
- "This Girl Is a Woman Now" (Gary Puckett & The Union Gap)
- "Sweet Caroline" (Neil Diamond)
- "Tracy" (I don't know who sings it; it's new.)

The bottom three:

- "Little Woman" (Bobby Sherman)
- "Sugar, Sugar" (The Archies)
- "The Train" (1910 Fruitgum Company)

I hear Ryan coming home from Shop-Rite. My parents went to bed an hour ago, so there shouldn't be any arguing tonight. I pull on some shorts and walk downstairs.

"What's happening, brother?" he says. He's got the refrigerator open and is fishing around for something to eat. He takes out a plate of roast beef from Sunday covered in foil, sniffs it, and puts it back. He opens the freezer and pulls out a Fudgsicle. "Want one?"

"Sure."

He sits on the couch in the family room, and I take the love seat. We leave the light on in the kitchen but leave the family room dark.

He sighs loudly, then takes a bite out of the fudge bar. "Tonight was a drag," he says. "And why am I eating ice cream? I spent the past eight hours going in and out of a walk-in freezer. I practically have frostbite."

"Mets got rained out," I say. "They play two tomorrow."

He nods. "They're doing good," he says, but he sounds distracted.

My fudge bar starts to drip, so I put about half of it in my mouth and run to get a napkin. I bring him one, too.

I've got that new song going through my head, and I've only heard it twice. *Tracy . . . da da da da.* Hmm. It's catchy.

We're quiet for several minutes. I can't remember any more words, but the few that I do keep running over and over in my mind.

Ryan says, "Damn," barely loud enough to hear.

"You all right?"

"Yeah," he says. "A little bummed out. . . . Sort of confused."

"Me, too."

He laughs lightly. "What are you confused about?"

"I don't know. . . . You going to that dance Thursday?"

He shakes his head. "Working till eleven every night this week."

"Oh."

"You thinking of going?" he asks.

"Thinking, yeah."

"You should."

"I don't know."

Ryan is a great dancer, or at least an energetic one. A few years ago he stayed home from school one day because he was sick or something. And when I got home at lunchtime, he was dancing in the family room to an Elvis record, jumping up and down and swinging his arms and his head.

The house behind our yard has a sloping driveway, and you can see straight across to it from the big picture windows in our family room. So I looked over there, and about eight kids—Jerry Ashenberg, Ramon Hernandez, at least two of the Foleys—were in the driveway laughing and pointing, probably more amazed than anything. Ryan waved and kept dancing. He didn't care.

I hear some thunder. That's the pattern lately: hot all day, threats of rain late at night. Ryan wraps his ice-cream stick in the napkin and lies back, hanging his feet over the end of the couch.

I don't know how much to ask him. He's always been the one I go to with problems, way more than I'd go to Mom or Dad. I know he's troubled, but how much could I help him?

"So, what are *you* confused about?" I ask.

"Stuff. Turning eighteen, mostly."

"Yeah. . . . I know."

There's another long silence. That's okay; we're thinking.

"I mean, I want to go to college," he says, "but *eventually*. Not because somebody almost literally has a gun to my head. If they'd end the frickin' war, this wouldn't be an issue. You know?"

"Yeah, I guess."

"I mean, that's some hell of a choice—go study economics or basket-weaving for four years, or get your head blown off in Southeast Asia. Nice priorities."

I swallow. I lie back, too.

"It's not even like we have a right to be there," he says. "Frickin' Nixon. Frickin' war mongrel."

That's the last thing we say for a while. I stare at the ceiling for five minutes. There's more thunder and I can see a few streaks of lightning off in the distance. I shut my eyes.

I should go upstairs. Turn on the radio and see if they'll play that "Tracy" song again so I can get some of the lyrics down. Four words is all I've got.

"See, you have to think for yourself," Ryan says. "This 'my country, right or wrong' crap doesn't make us better; it makes us stupid."

It sounds like he's talking out loud to himself, but that isn't like him. I guess he's talking to both of us, testing out his theories. "Don't follow the flock if they're leading you over a cliff," he says.

"I hear you." I have no idea what it'd be like to face the end of what I know. To get shipped halfway across the world and put myself in the direct path of somebody's gun—a lot of people's guns and bombs and grenades.

Ryan nods off on the couch, and I just watch him snore. He's fidgety in his sleep, and I don't remember him ever being like that. We always used to sleep like babies here, safe in this house and in this town. I never even thought about being in danger before. I doubt he did either, at least not before this year. I haven't had a good night's sleep in a month.

I won't quit football. How could I wimp out of something like that when I compare it to what Ryan's facing?

And that dance, too. I'm going. I've been thinking about Patty, even though I try not to. Not about making out with her or showing off by walking along the Boulevard with her; just about that hint of a smile she shows me sometimes. Just that possibility that she likes me. I think she's just shy.

I could see it happening. We're at the dance and she tells me she's had a crush on me all summer. That she's so excited to finally be alone with me.

I could definitely see it happening.

It's almost starting to feel urgent.

Urgent that I *make* something happen. Not with her, specifically, or on the football field or whatever. Just something. Something big.

Because you never know when it'll be too late. When you might eat your last hot dog, or get sent to Vietnam, or wake up and find out you're dead.

TUESDAY, AUGUST 26:

Pushing the Limit

Five laps today, which is at least a mile. Me and Tony race to the front and get way ahead of everybody—they're all either tired from scrimmaging or slow. But we cut the pace after one lap, running comfortably enough to talk but also fast enough so the coaches won't yell at us.

"You been working on your moves?" Tony asks.

"What moves?" I haven't touched the ball since that fumble.

"For Thursday night."

"Oh." I make a hard turn and cut through the end zone. "I know how to dance; I don't have to practice." That isn't true at all, but I don't plan to do any dancing anyway.

"Not dance moves," he says. "You know, after, when we're walking them home."

I hadn't thought about that. Nobody said anything about walking them home. We don't even know if they'll show up. Or if any of us will get into the dance.

We finish the second lap. A few of the linemen are just a short distance ahead of us, finishing their first.

"You might as well try," Tony says. "See if you can get anywhere with her. At least kiss her for a few seconds."

I'm not sure which one he means by "her." Or where this great make-out scene might take place.

"If nothing else, you gotta split her off from Patty for me," he says. "Get me some alone time."

"So you'll be with Patty, huh?"

"Whataya think? I'm the one who set this thing up, so I get the . . . so I get Patty."

And I get Janet. Nothing wrong with her, but I'm seeing it differently. No way Patty likes Tony. I don't know what she thinks of me, but all I see when she has to look at Tony is disgust.

I start running a little faster now. He keeps up, but I can tell that he's starting to breathe harder.

"What I'm hoping to do is take them over to the Little League fields," he says. The fields are adjacent to the swim club.

"You planning to play baseball?" I intend it as a joke, but he just sneers.

"Dugouts are nice and secluded, especially at night." He holds up his right hand and makes some squeezing motions.

I go faster and move five yards ahead of him. I'm not in the mood for his daydreaming.

"Who you racing?" he says.

I glance over my shoulder. "Come on." And I turn the heat up even more.

I can hear him panting now, trying to catch me. But I'm pulling away from him. After four laps he's thirty yards behind, and I run the last one at full speed, lapping almost everybody else on the team.

Nobody seems to notice, as usual.

Tony doesn't say anything after he joins me on the sideline, where I'm waiting for everybody else to finish. He's got his hands on his knees and he coughs a couple of times. I could run five more laps.

Coach yells at some of the linemen as they finish and try to sit down. "Walk it off!" he says. "We got too many people close to the limit. I don't want any surprises on Saturday."

The weight limit for our division is 140 pounds, and I'd say at least three guys are pushing that. Anybody questionable gets weighed in front of the referees and coaches from both teams a half hour before the kickoff. If you're over, you don't play.

"So we'll be running all week," Coach says as we huddle up. "East Rutherford is big, they're fast, they're tough, and they're our rivals. Without total concentration, we'll get our butts kicked."

Me and Tony walk off with Colaneri and Delcalzo. "We beat East Rutherford by three touchdowns last year," Colaneri says when we're out of earshot of the coaches. "He's just trying to psych us up."

"Hope it's at least that much this year," Tony says to me. "Otherwise we get no playing time."

"We get kickoffs," I say.

"Yeah, but that ain't the same as running the ball."

I still have my helmet on, so I undo the chin strap and lift it off my head. I'm not so sure I want to be running the ball after that fumble last weekend. Imagine doing that in front of a Saturday night crowd at home.

The steps at Corpus Christi are empty this time. We stop across the street and Tony looks up and down the Boulevard. Then he does it again.

"We should wait," he says.

"What for?"

He looks at me in disbelief. "We must be early. They'll show."

"We're actually later than usual," I say. "All those laps."

"Then I guess we missed 'em."

"It's not like they sit there waiting for us every day."

"Often enough," he says.

"Once. And that was probably a coincidence."

"No, it wasn't. You don't understand anything."

"No. You don't." I start walking home. He stays where he is.

"Give it five minutes," he says.

"I'm hungry."

"So am I. But some things are bigger than that."

I stop walking and face him, fifteen feet away. "They aren't here."

"They will be."

I sweep my hand toward the church steps. "So go ahead and wait. I'm leaving." And I walk another ten feet.

I look back and he's still standing there with his mouth hanging open. I turn and start walking again. After two blocks I hear him running up behind me.

"They didn't show," he says, as if that's news.

"No kidding."

"Must have got delayed somewhere," he says. "I thought they'd be there."

"Why would you think that?"

"They wait there for us every day."

"Once," I say again. "And who says they were waiting for us?"

He shakes his head. "Man, you don't understand anything. . . . You just don't get it at all."

WEDNESDAY, AUGUST 27:

Mister Salty

The Mets are on television tonight. Mom's out at a library board meeting, so me and Dad and Ryan camp out in the family room to watch.

We've got a low table in front of the couch, and Dad sets a box of saltines and a jar of green olives there. We munch our way through them by the end of the first inning. Koosman gives up a solo homer in the bottom of the inning, so the Padres take a rare lead.

Dad comes back with Ritz crackers and a slab of cheddar cheese for the second inning, slicing it with a big knife with a black handle. I eat a few crackers, but I don't like cheese, so I get the jar of peanut butter after the Mets go down, and spread that on 'em.

Koosman gets the Mets' first hit in the top of the third (the Mets have the best-hitting pitchers in the league), then Agee walks. Cleon Jones doubles them both home, and the Mets take the lead.

"Looking good," Dad says. "Been a lot of years since there was a New York baseball team to get excited about."

Ryan goes to the cellar for drinks. "Brody!" he yells from downstairs. "What kind you want?"

I try to envision what's in there. I know there's lemon (that's all Mom drinks) and I'm pretty sure there's some root beer. "Any grape?"

I hear Ryan moving cans around. "No!"

"Then orange."

"Okay."

He comes back with a Rheingold and two Shop-Rite sodas.

"What kind of pretzels we got out there?" Dad calls as Ryan enters the kitchen.

I hear a cabinet swing open. "Mister Salty."

"Bring 'em on."

The drinks and the pretzels cover us for a few innings. It occurs to me that the Padres haven't had a base runner since the first.

"Koosman is having an incredible stretch of games," Dad says. "Seaver, too. And pitching wins championships."

Art Shamsky doubles in a run for the Mets in the sixth, then scores on Ken Boswell's single.

"Of course, it doesn't hurt to have hitters," Dad says. He gets up and heads to the bathroom.

Mom comes home from her meeting and sits next to Ryan on the love seat. "Exciting game?" she asks. She never pays any attention to professional sports. She did show up for all of my Little League games and Ryan's basketball games, though.

"Hi, honey," Dad says. He's in the kitchen, standing in front of the open freezer. He comes back with a dish of coffee ice cream.

Mom yawns. "Guess I'll read in bed," she says.

Koosman hits the leadoff batter with a pitch in the bottom of the sixth, but the Mets immediately turn a double play.

"No contest," Dad says. "Man, I wish my father could see this team. He was a huge Yankees fan back in the day. DiMaggio, Yogi, Johnny Mize." He shakes his head. His father dropped dead shoveling snow.

Ryan picks up the olive jar. "Better put this back," he says. He goes to the kitchen.

"There might be a beer in there," Dad says.

Ryan shifts some bottles around in the refrigerator. "Nope. I'll get you one."

This time he comes up with two of them and pops one open.

Dad eats another pretzel. "What else we got out there?" he asks Ryan.

Ryan shrugs. "I didn't notice."

"What good are you?"

I smile. "Mom bought another watermelon."

They both laugh.

"Now that sounds good," Dad says.

"Yeah!" Ryan adds. "Let's scarf it down."

So Dad gets three massive slices and a big handful of napkins. "No juice on the upholstery," he warns.

"I better get us some plates," I say. So I do.

Koosman hits another single, but they leave him stranded. By the time it's over he's pitched the last eight and a third without yielding a hit. The Mets are looking dominant, but again, this is the Padres we're talking about.

The game ends and we sit there grinning. Dad gets up and switches to channel 11. The intro to *The Honeymooners* is just coming on, Jackie Gleason's face in the moon.

"Awesome," Ryan says.

"Funniest thing on television," Dad says. "These shows are fifteen years old, and nobody's come close."

They both take a swig of their beers. I go to the cellar for another can of soda, and we laugh our heads off for another half hour.

Nothing like summer. Too bad it's almost over.

THURSDAY, AUGUST 28:

Nothing to Lose

The swim club closes at seven o'clock so they can set things up for the dance. We decided that instead of trying to get by the authorities at the gate, we would slip into the locker room just before closing and hide in a shower stall.

Tony pulls the dark plastic curtain closed. We're in a space about four feet by four.

"Not a word," he whispers.

I nod. "This is going to be a long hour."

"It'll be worth it." He leans against the cinder-block wall with his arms folded. There's no room to sit down. Even if we could, the floor is slimy. So we just stand there waiting.

After about fifteen minutes a lifeguard walks through the locker room and calls, "Everybody out?"

There's no response, so he leaves. Tony raises one fist and gives me a smug smile. Looks like we're safe.

Eventually we can hear the band tuning up—a few twangs

on an electric guitar and some drumbeats. Somebody comes in to use a urinal, so we hold our breath and stand like statues.

The plan is to wait until we hear some actual songs, so we're certain the dance has started. Then we'll just walk out real casually and get lost in the crowd. Tony claims that he ran into Janet and Patty this afternoon and said we'd meet them behind the diving boards, but I don't know when he could have done that. We hung out together from late in the morning until two thirty, then went home, changed, and went to football practice. And we walked home together, too, with no sign of them anywhere.

So, unless they're hiding out in the girls' shower stalls, I don't have a ton of confidence that they'll be here.

There are probably a hundred kids standing around the basketball court when we finally dare to come out. Some of them are our age. The band is playing "Midnight Confessions," but nobody's dancing. There's a steady stream of people coming through the gate.

We see free soda and cookies on a table by the shuffleboard court, so we head over there and get cups of Coke. Then we walk the inner perimeter of the grounds a few times, like we do every day when we come here. A few people are swimming.

Patty and Janet walk in with a bunch of older girls. They're both wearing sleeveless dresses and choker beads.

"Let's go," Tony says. He sets his empty cup on a bench and starts walking straight toward them.

"Hey," he says as we reach them.

Janet smiles and flicks up her eyebrows. Patty just stares at us. She's got her hair up some.

"So you got in," Tony says, lowering his voice. "Any hassle?"

Janet shakes her head. "We just breezed past."

"Nobody even looked at us," Patty says, glancing around at the band and the pool and the people. She's rotating her shoulders with the music. "They just took the money."

"Yeah," he says. "Us, too."

Patty finally meets my eyes, then quickly looks away. We start walking toward the band, and we stay there for a while and listen. Maybe ten people have started dancing, most of them girls.

Tony keeps trying to stand next to Patty, but she keeps moving away from him and winds up next to me instead.

"We should dance," Janet says eventually.

I take a half step back, but Tony follows them onto the blacktop. Janet and Patty start dancing, and Tony watches them. After a minute or so he dances, too, cutting between them.

Tony's all arms, not moving his feet any, but he's bouncing his torso around pretty good. Patty keeps shifting away from him, and finally he gives up and faces Janet. After the song ends, Patty walks off and stands next to me again. I think she still looks shy.

"You don't dance?" she asks.

"Yeah," I say. "Just wasn't ready."

She shrugs.

We watch Janet and Tony dance to two more songs. I figure I have nothing to lose, so when the next one starts I say, "You wanna?" and point toward Tony and Janet.

She smiles slightly for the first time tonight, and we walk over. They're playing "All You Need Is Love," which is kind of slow, so I don't have to do much. The next one is fast, so me and Tony walk off while the girls keep dancing. They seem to be having a lot more fun without us.

"This is setting up just right," Tony says.

"What is?"

He nudges me with his elbow. "For later."

I don't know how he figures that. Patty hasn't even acknowledged him.

"Change in plans," he says. "As soon as it's dark"—that would be in less than half an hour—"we bring 'em over by the swings. Then I take her for a walk back in the picnic area, and you get lost."

"You take *who* for a walk?"

"Janet. Who do you think?"

"You said Patty before."

"No, I didn't."

"Yes, you did."

"Well, I changed my mind."

He had it changed for him. But that works in my favor anyway, so I'm not arguing.

Not that I'm expecting anything to happen.

The girls dance for about twenty minutes. Me and Tony get more soda and lean against the chain-link fence. The band gets louder.

They finally walk over to us. Janet grabs Tony's soda and drinks the last half of it. She wipes her forehead with her hand. "We're sweating," she says. She tilts her head toward the locker rooms, and she and Patty walk off together.

"It's time to take advantage of this situation," Tony says. The girls' locker room is on the way to the swings, so we follow about thirty feet behind them and wait till they come out.

"Take a break?" Tony asks when they reappear.

"Sure," Janet says.

"Hit the swings?"

"Okay."

It's dark and much quieter over on this side of the grounds. We sit on the swings.

"Can't dance too much," Tony says. "We got our opening game in two days. Coach would be pissed if we tired ourselves out dancing."

Janet says, "I see." Patty yawns.

"We'll be out there for the opening kickoff," Tony continues. "First play. Starting lineup."

"Kickoff team only," I say. "We're not exactly starters."

"Who's on the field when the game starts?" he says. "The *starters*. You can't argue against that."

Janet starts pumping her legs a little to get moving on the swing.

"Let me give you a push," Tony says. He stands behind her and gives her back a shove. After two more pushes he steps out of the way and she starts going pretty high. Patty gets going on her own. They're giggling.

Janet stops first. Tony seizes the opportunity and pulls on her arm. "I wanna show you something," he says.

"What?"

"Over there." He points toward Route 17. The back corner of the grounds is just as dark as it is around the swings. There's a huge old maple tree in the corner.

They walk off. Patty slows quickly and hops off the swing. "Where are you guys going?"

"We'll be right back," Tony calls.

I figure I'll play along and try to get Tony some privacy. "You must be dying of thirst after all that dancing," I say.

Patty stares after Tony and Janet with a frown, but then she says, "Yeah. I am." So we get more cups of soda.

We start wandering with the cups, passing the locker rooms and the swings. She hasn't said anything about Janet, but I'm sure she's eager to see what's going on, so she heads that way. When we reach the kiddie pool I say, "Hold on." I sit on a bench and yank off my sneaker, stalling for time.

"Got a rock or something in here," I say, shaking the shoe. I put it back on. She's sitting now, too.

"I wonder what's so interesting over there," she says,

smirking a little and jutting her head toward the dark corner where Tony and Janet went.

"Tony's into trees," I say. "He wants to study them in college."

"Uh-huh. What else does he want to study?" She laughs.

"Right." I inch closer to her. "Nice night, huh?"

She looks at the sky. "Yeah. Fun." She closes her eyes and inhales deeply. Mostly what you smell over here is chlorine.

I slide my hand along the bench and hesitate. It's not as if she's never made out with anybody, so I lift my hand and set it on her back. She wiggles slightly, then turns and looks at me hard. "What are you doing?"

"Nothing." I pull my hand away in a hurry.

She stands up. "I gotta find Janet."

I stand up, too. Janet is walking toward us. She's smiling.

"Where've you been?" Patty asks.

"Back there." Janet looks directly at me. "You might want to go help your friend," she says. "I think I knocked him out."

Patty laughs and they walk off together. I hear her say "Jerks!" I head for the corner.

Tony is just a few yards away, on the other side of the kiddie pool. He's rubbing his jaw.

"She punch you?" I ask.

He puts a finger to his tongue, then pulls it away and looks at it. It's pretty dark over here, but I can tell that there isn't any blood.

"Just once," he says. He laughs. "I didn't know where to stop."

"I guess she let you know."

"Yeah, she did."

We sit on the same bench I'd been on with Patty.

"So what happened?" I ask.

"She let me kiss her a couple of times. It was good. Then I got my hands up too high. I said it was a mistake. The second time I did it she belted me."

I crack up. He does, too.

"So how'd you do?" he asks.

"I didn't get punched."

"That's good. Let's get out of here. I've had enough for one night."

"Let's go."

We pass through the gate and head up the hill. We stop near the Little League fields and look back at the basketball court. It's fairly full now; most people are dancing. We can see Patty and Janet out there, too.

If it wasn't for Tony, I never would have come here. No way. It didn't work out so good, but I guess I'm glad I came.

Tony has no idea what he's doing, but I gotta give him credit. He was definitely in there trying.

Thirty-two Hours Away

I watch game shows and old comedies all morning. *I Love Lucy*, *Gilligan's Island*, *Concentration*. I eat two bowls of cereal, a grape ice pop, and a peanut butter sandwich.

"So you had fun last night?" Mom asks.

"I guess. Sort of."

"Did you dance with anybody special?"

Does she really think I'd answer that even if I had? "Tony's pretty special."

"You know what I mean."

"I don't know how to dance."

She puts her hand on top of my head and strokes my hair. "You'll learn. This is a big year for you, Brody. Junior high school can be intimidating, but you'll do fine. Just be yourself."

"Who else would I be?"

"Oh," she says with a laugh, "kids your age try to be all kinds of people. You'll see."

I sink lower into the couch.

"I have some good news," she says. "I found out who your teacher is."

"You did?" We're not supposed to know until the first day of school.

"Mmm-hmm. It's Mrs. Wilkey. Same teacher Ryan had."

"Oh." I figure Mom found that out at the library meeting the other night. There are teachers on the board with her.

"You'll love her," Mom says. "She's very nice."

She's also very old, and according to Ryan she wasn't nice at all. We'll see. I've had some teachers before who'd had Ryan first. Sometimes it's good and sometimes it isn't, depending on how much of a pain he was at the time.

Football's got me worried. It's been a while since I carried the ball, but those fumbles are haunting me. What'll it be like out there under the lights, with everybody watching, in an actual game with everything on the line? I'm scared to death I'll screw up, miss a tackle on a kickoff, and be responsible for a big runback.

Game time is thirty-two hours away, and there's no way I can stand this kind of pressure until then. So I grab a basketball and head out to the driveway to shoot.

I'm thinking about trying out for the Franklin basketball team, but that'll be mostly eighth graders and I'll be at a size disadvantage. But I'm *always* at a disadvantage, so that's nothing new.

Anyway, I've got an entire football season to get through first.

I can shoot. At least here in the driveway. Ryan says our

basket is probably three or four inches too low, but we've never measured it.

I take a long shot and it swishes through the net. I sprint in and follow it with a layup, then dribble out to the foul line and hit another.

I'm wondering what it must have felt like for Tony when he kissed Janet last night. However good it must have felt, it was probably overcome by that punch to the face he got afterward. I imagine his lip is puffy today.

Guess that could have been me, since Tony's original plan had him winding up with Patty. Then again, maybe that's what Patty wanted. Maybe she would have kissed him, too. And instead of just a nasty reply from Patty, I would have been the one getting belted by Janet.

But either way, I definitely had the whole thing wrong in my head. That summer-long crush I hoped Patty had on me turned out to be anything but. I felt about seven years old when she called us jerks.

I don't feel any different than I did a year ago, when I was heading into sixth grade. I have no idea what goes on inside girls' heads. I don't have any idea what goes on inside guys' heads, either, at least not the cool ones.

What's inside my head right now is nervousness and embarrassment. Good combination.

Franklin School, here I come.

Unnecessary Roughness

I look pretty good in the game jersey. I'm all suited up by four forty-five for the seven o'clock game. Tony finally comes by, and we walk down to the field. His lip doesn't look any worse than mine did last week.

"You scared?" he asks me.

"What for?" I'm sure he can tell that I am.

"Me, too," he says. "But I can't wait to make that first hit. Just nail somebody on the opening kickoff, you know? Knock all the nerves right out of my system."

"That would work."

But we win the coin toss and decide to receive the ball, so we won't be kicking off after all. We stand on the sidelines and watch.

East Rutherford is apparently better than they were a year ago. The game is scoreless at halftime. We spent the first half standing off to the side, yelling but not really feeling like part of the team.

Tony grabs my sleeve as we walk out of the locker room for the second half. "Nice and clean," he says.

"Won't be for long," I say. Now we'll be kicking off.

East Rutherford has a fast running back who almost broke a couple in the second quarter. Number 33. He's back deep for the kick, so we're wary.

Mitchell's kick is high and relatively short, and it drifts toward my side of the field. One of the midfield players circles back and catches it, and he immediately swings toward the opposite sideline. I do my box-in around the thirty; otherwise the whole play would be past me. Everybody else from our team is heading toward the return man.

But suddenly 33 is coming toward me with the ball.

"Reverse!" somebody yells.

The guy cuts sharply up the middle of the field as he draws even with me, but I'm ten yards from him. The field is wide open.

I pivot and start angling toward him at full speed. There's no way I'll catch him without help, but I can see Mitchell heading toward him from the opposite side. So the guy gives a head fake and hesitates just slightly, veering into my path. I lunge and wrap both arms around his churning legs, and Mitchell hits him high.

I saved a touchdown, but they're at our forty-two. I get to my knees and hop up. My teammates are clapping as I run off the field. Magrini punches my arm.

Coach Epstein smacks me lightly on the shoulder pad and says, "Nice job!"

Ferrante holds out a palm and I meet it.

My heart is beating ferociously, and my breathing is short and hard. That's excitement, not fatigue. I stand closer to the coaches now, a foot back from the sideline.

Unfortunately, all I did was postpone the touchdown, because they drive down the field with a solid running game. Number 33 takes it the last seven yards to the end zone.

But they get greedy. They try the same play to the other side for the conversion, and Magrini reads it well. He drops the guy for a loss, so the score stays 6–0.

"Get it right back!" Coach Epstein says. He grabs Ferrante's arm and whispers intensely to him while East Rutherford kicks off.

I take a deep breath and let it out, then glance at the scoreboard. Plenty of time. We're not even midway through the third quarter.

But the clock moves quickly. We keep the ball on the ground, getting four first downs but nothing substantial.

The crowd's been quiet. Even the cheerleaders have been standing and watching.

Finally we've got a fourth-and-four at the East Rutherford twenty-one. Way too far for a field goal attempt. Ferrante hands off to Esposito, who's hit in the backfield but manages to roll off, breaking toward the sideline. A linebacker hits him hard. Esposito twists and reaches for the first down. The officials call for a measurement.

Esposito comes up holding his leg, limping around. The officials stretch out the chains, and I can see that we're about three inches short. The crowd groans.

Coach grabs Colaneri and sends him in at cornerback for Esposito, who hobbles off the field.

We get the ball back with five minutes left in the game.

"Kenny, you ready to go?" Coach calls to Esposito, who's been sitting on the bench.

"Yes." He stands and puts on his helmet and runs onto the field. You can tell that he's wincing, but he barrels through the line four times in a row, moving us past midfield.

"Think we'll ever pass?" Tony says softly to me.

"We might not need to."

The next time Esposito goes down, he stays down. The ref calls time-out and our coaches walk onto the field. Coach Powell pulls Kenny up a minute later and helps him off the field.

"Ankle," Tony says.

"Looks like it."

I guess we've softened up the East Rutherford line, because Colaneri picks up where Esposito left off, gaining four or five yards a carry and eating up the clock.

Ferrante drops back with the ball. He's thrown only one pass all game, so East Rutherford has its defenders packed in. Lorenzo is wide open, and he catches the pass and runs untouched into the end zone.

We erupt. The cheerleaders start that "Rah rah Eddie

Lorenzo" thing. Then they do one for Ferrante. After that they have to do one for Mitchell, too, because he just kicked the extra point to put us in the lead.

I jump up with both fists in the air.

"Let's go!" Tony says, running onto the field.

I'd pretty much forgotten that we have to kick off.

We huddle up. "Don't get fooled again!" Mitchell yells. "This is the game."

I look at the scoreboard: HOME 7, VISITOR 6. TIME REMAINING: 1:28.

The kick goes to number 33 again. He runs straight, then starts to drift to my side. I get hit hard as I begin to box, but I roll off the block and keep my feet, stumbling backward. I dig in and find my balance just as 33 moves into my area. Two other guys hit him and stop his progress. I dive into the pile to make sure.

The whistle blows as I stand up, and I see a yellow flag flying through the air.

The referee points at me, then signals to the bench. "Unnecessary roughness, number 27, blue. Fifteen yards."

Coach Epstein has his arms folded as I jog to the sideline, and he's shaking his head. "Winslow weighs fifty pounds," he mutters. "Unnecessary roughness?"

I'm fuming. I stand with my back to the crowd, helmet on. That could cost us the game.

"Stupid move," I say as Tony stops next to me.

"That was nothing," he replies. "You didn't hurt nobody."

"Except the team," I say. "I knew he was down. I just couldn't stop myself."

"We'll be fine. We'll stop 'em."

But 33 dashes toward the sideline on a pitchout and races right past us. Colaneri knocks him out of bounds near the thirty.

Still a minute left.

They split two ends out to the right, and the quarterback drops back. We've got good coverage, so he throws a short one over the middle. It's complete, but the play eats up a lot of time.

They run one, then call time-out. It's third down.

A long pass falls incomplete. Fourth-and-two at the twenty-three. Thirty-four seconds left.

"It'd be a forty-yard field goal," Tony says.

"No way. They didn't even kick the extra point. They have to go for it."

Magrini and Lorenzo chase the quarterback around the backfield. He keeps scrambling, but nobody's open. Magrini sacks him and the ball comes loose. Lorenzo falls on it. That's the game.

We shake hands at midfield, then run all the way to the locker room, shouting and jumping.

Coach tells us we played great. That we'll keep playing conservatively and won't run anybody off the field. That a win is a win.

"Where's Winslow?" he says, looking around.

I put up my hand.

"Don't be so rough on those poor guys," he says, laughing. "You don't want to break anybody in half out there. . . . Seriously, good effort. Everybody played hard. Let's keep at it. And don't be shy about hitting people. Penalties are part of the game."

And I was part of the game, too. Two plays, but they both were meaningful.

My first real game. I'll take it.

SUNDAY, AUGUST 31

Before the Kickoff

By Brody Winslow

At game time you feel like puking
Or diarrhea in your pants
Because everybody's watching
And you might just blow your chance
And be embarrassed by your screwup
And the bonehead play you made
It's a lot like thinking forward
To the start of seventh grade

MONDAY, SEPTEMBER 1:

The Upper Hand

Labor Day. Last day of the season at the swim club; last day of freedom before school starts. No practice, at least, so we wait until late afternoon to go to the pool. It's packed.

My father almost never goes to the swim club, since he's in Manhattan every weekday and usually messes around the house with projects all weekend. But he finished retiling and caulking around the tub yesterday, so Mom convinced him to take today off.

He sits under the umbrella with yesterday's *New York Times* and today's *Herald-News*, slowly eating roasted peanuts from a jar. His body is pale and hairy. The hair cuts off in a straight line at the middle of his calves, though, rubbed away from wearing tight, black nylon socks all day at work. So it's like he's wearing flesh-tone socks instead.

They have adult swims for fifteen minutes every hour all day, so he does some laps then. Me and Tony sit on the edge of the pool with our legs hanging in.

"Tomorrow's gonna be bad," Tony says.

"Why you think that?"

"They say seventh is a hundred times harder than sixth. You get huge amounts of homework, and the teachers expect you to act like adults."

"Yeah." I've heard that, too. You stay in one classroom for a lot of the time, but you switch out for science and art and shop. Some other things, too, I think. Maybe health. Music.

"They put the meanest teachers at Franklin," Tony says. "You have to be *sort* of nice to teach elementary, and the best teachers go to the high school. So that leaves the worst ones for junior high."

"Makes sense."

My father swims over and grabs my legs. "Hey, Nimrod," he says.

"How's the water?" I ask. We haven't been in yet. Of course, I've got my legs in there. It's just something you say.

"Delicious," he replies. He swims away on his back.

"How many different names does he have for you?" Tony asks.

"Unlimited."

I look across the pool and see Patty and Janet staring at us. They look at each other and laugh.

I can feel my face getting hot. I elbow Tony and point my chin over there.

He smiles. "They see us yet?" he asks.

"They were looking right at us."

"That's good. This ain't over yet."

I kick at the water. I've been hoping that it was.

"We'll just ignore 'em for now," he says. "But believe me, we'll get another chance. She was liking that as much as I was."

"Yeah, especially the punch."

He tests his jaw again. "That was just for show, so I wouldn't get too confident. She wanted to keep the upper hand for now. But it's shifting."

"How do you know?"

"I just do. I got a good instinct for this sort of thing. She'll let me know when she's ready."

"And where does that leave me? I'm supposed to run interference for you again?"

"Maybe to start. Depends on the situation. You'll be all right. Patty's just a little shyer than Janet is. Next time around you'll do better."

I look across the pool again. They're sitting on a bench. Patty doesn't look shy anymore. She looks mean.

The adult swim ends. Dad swims over and says, "You hungry, Idjit?"

"Yeah. What we got?"

"Your mother packed chicken and some other stuff. Tony, you're welcome to join us."

We head for the picnic area. Dad pops open a Rheingold, and we eat cold chicken legs and homemade coleslaw.

"Last day of being little kids," Dad says with his mouth full. "Eat up."

I can tell he's joking, but there's a lot of truth in that, too. I have no idea what this school year will be like.

"You guys stay little as long as you want to," Mom says. "You'll be teenagers before you know it. Enjoy your innocence while you have it."

I glance at Tony. He's got a sly look on his face. He picks up a napkin and wipes his mouth, then reaches for another chicken leg. "These are great, Mrs. Winslow," he says.

"Have all you want. There's plenty."

When we leave the picnic area, Janet and Patty are on the swings, so we have to walk right past them. I move to the outside of Mom and Dad, so they'll be between me and the girls. Tony comes over to my side, too.

We hear them laughing after we're past. Tony looks back.

"Just a little shy," he whispers. "Believe me, they'll let us know when they're ready."

TUESDAY, SEPTEMBER 2:

Yap-Yaps

Mrs. Wilkey spends the first hour of school deciding where people should sit. Mostly she bases it on height (I'm not the shortest boy, but it's close, so I get the second seat in the second row), but she also says she wants the "wise guys" near the front. She doesn't know any of us, but I guess after a hundred years of teaching seventh graders she can quickly identify the troublemakers.

They apparently include Magrini and Finken, who she places in the first and second seats in the row in front of her desk.

We have to take our seats as soon as they're assigned to us so she can mull over the people who are still standing. I turn to the girl in the seat next to me. She appears to be amused about the seating ritual.

"I'm Diane," she says.

I've never seen her before, but that's true of a lot of the kids who went to Lincoln.

"You?" she asks.

"Brody. Winslow. I went to Euclid."

"I figured that." She has longish dark hair. She smiles as if she's sure of who she is, not like some of these other good-looking girls who just stare right past me, looking for a guy with status to help prop up their egos. She's cute.

Very cute.

"Good class," she says. "Should be fun."

Mrs. Wilkey stops what she's doing and points at her. "Miss?"

"Diane."

"Diane, in this classroom, you only speak when called upon."

"So are you calling on me now?"

"No, I am not. I'm telling you to be quiet."

Mrs. Wilkey goes back to the seating assignments. Diane crosses her arms and leans back in her chair. When Mrs. Wilkey has her back turned, she sticks her tongue out at her. Then she smiles again, right at me.

I point my finger at her and carefully and deliberately mouth those same words. "I'm telling you to be quiet."

This time she sticks her tongue out at me.

Seventh grade seems to be off to a good start.

We get hauled up to the auditorium after a while so the principal can hit us with the rules. The auditorium is on the third floor, and only two classes at a time are allowed up there. Technically, the auditorium isn't quite condemned, but the roof leaks and there's some question about how solid the floor is. So a room built for a couple of hundred people isn't supposed to hold more than fifty now.

The principal seems cross and sort of confused. He repeats things. At first I thought it was for emphasis, but the third time he tells us about not running in the halls, somebody from the other class raises his hand.

The kid's from Lincoln, so I don't know him. He stands and says, "Are we allowed to run in the halls?"

Everybody laughs. The principal says, "No, you are not."

That class's teacher—Mr. Enright—walks to the end of the aisle and motions to the kid with his finger. The kid gets up and shuffles over. The teacher makes him sit way in the back by himself.

I'm sitting next to Finken. He leans toward me and says, "That's Danny Pellegrini. That whole class is a bunch of yap-yaps. They barely got out of Lincoln."

"Yeah. Same with the Euclid kids. That was funny, though."

"Oh, he's hilarious, just not very bright."

When we get back to the classroom, Finken calls me over to his desk. He opens the lid and points to one of the many names carved into the underside.

"You know this guy?" he asks.

It says *Ryan Winslow*.

"That's my brother."

"Cool. When was that?"

"Six years ago."

Mrs. Wilkey is the last one into the room. She fires me a look and says, "Take your seat, young man."

I walk over. Diane is looking at me. When she's sure Mrs. Wilkey isn't watching, she mouths "young man" at me with a stern look. Then she laughs.

We have to hustle home after school so we can suit up and get to practice by four.

"How'd it go?" Tony asks me.

"Pretty good. Good class."

"Mine stinks," he says. "How did I wind up in the smart class?"

"Beats me," I say. "Somebody made a mistake."

"Ha-ha. You know what I mean. We got all the straight-A students. What fun is that?"

"You must have been left over or something. You know, all the classes were even except the smart one, so they just threw the last guy in there."

"I come way before you in the alphabet," he says. "You should be in Mr. Blaine's class."

"Because I'm smart?"

"No, because your name starts with W."

"You'll be all right," I say. "You'll just have to study a couple of extra hours every night. It'll be fun."

"Sure it will."

"You got homework already?"

"Tons of it," he says. "We have to read like ten pages in social studies and do a page of math problems."

"We just have to cover our books."

"We gotta do that, too. It's insane."

We walk past Euclid. Tony could stay with me for another block, but it's quicker for him if he turns here.

"How's the girl situation?" he asks.

"Where?"

"In your class."

"I don't know. Regular."

"*Regular*." He snorts. "Any prospects?"

"What do you care? What about Janet?"

"What about her? I ain't limiting myself."

"I'm not either."

I'm not saying a word to him about anybody in my classroom. Blaine's room is right across the hall, so Tony will see the situation. I don't want his help. He was no help at all with the other one.

He leaves, so I walk the last block alone. I'm feeling good. I started the day feeling intimidated, but something shifted. I felt like I fit in. There's power in numbers, I think. And we aren't little kids anymore.

The Turpentiney Rag

Ryan has a very small black-and-white TV in his room. The screen is about eight inches wide. *Frankenstein* is on at eleven thirty, and Mom and Dad told him it's okay to have Skippy and Jenny up here to watch it after work as long as it's very quiet. "So you don't disturb your little brother," Mom said.

They've gone to bed, so they don't know that I'm in here watching the movie, too.

We've got a huge bottle of birch beer and a bag of potato chips. All four of us sit on Ryan's bed, backs against the wall, facing the TV set.

Skippy holds up a small bottle of vodka and twirls it around. "Who wants some?" he asks.

Ryan and Jenny hold out their cups, and Skippy adds some to their soda.

During a commercial Jenny asks him if he has to work

tomorrow. Skippy got a job last week loading trucks somewhere over in Moonachie. He starts at six a.m.

"Yeah, but vodka helps me sleep," he says. "I only need like four hours a night."

I quickly calculate how much I get. I usually fall asleep around midnight, so I guess I average six on school nights and maybe seven on the weekends. It never seems like enough, but I definitely like staying up late. They play better music on the radio then, avoiding the really crappy songs most of the time. Plus I like sports talk, which is on late. Lots of nights I just stare out the window at New York City.

"How'd you like Mrs. Wilkey?" Ryan asks me.

Skippy answers before I can. "She hated my guts," he says.

"You didn't have her," Ryan says.

"I know. But she had my brother, Larry, like four years before I even got to Franklin, and she thought I was him whenever she saw me in the halls. He was there *four years* earlier. She'd say, 'Mr. Hankins, don't let me catch you leaving school early.'"

"Larry left school early?" Jenny asks.

"All the time. He'd go down to the Boulevard to buy cigarettes when they were supposed to be switching classes for science or something. Then he'd come back in time for the next class. But that had nothing to do with me. She wasn't even my teacher."

"Maybe she was trying to be funny," I say. She doesn't seem senile to me, just old.

"Who knows?" Skippy replies. "The whole two years I was at that school, she acted the same way. She even called me Larry sometimes."

The movie comes back on and we watch it silently until the next commercial. I grab a handful of potato chips.

Skippy snorts. "That's what you get for having a brother who's a troublemaker."

Ryan laughs. "Oh yeah. You *never* got in trouble."

"Not hardly," he says. "Three suspensions in seventh grade but only one in eighth. That's because I figured out how not to get caught."

"Doing what?" I ask.

"Smoking in the bathroom. Stealing supplies from the storage room. Stuff like that."

"What were the suspensions for?"

"Smoking twice. Once for setting a fire in shop. A very small fire. And it wasn't my fault."

"Whose was it?"

"Nobody's really. Just some turpentiney rag near my cigarette."

"Well," I say, "she seems all right to me. Lots of rules, but she doesn't pay much attention. Not so far, anyway."

"She liked me," Ryan says. "I don't know why. I always gave her a hard time. You're like that in seventh grade. There's nothing more boring than sitting there in class."

"You met me!" Jenny says.

"Yeah, but that didn't pay off for years," Ryan says with a laugh. "You thought I was an immature little jerk."

"You were!"

"No kidding." He holds out his cup and Skippy pours more vodka into it.

"You turned out okay," Jenny says. "The first day of class you tried to act really cool, like you were one of the 'it' crowd. I saw right through that. You were about as cool as a light-bulb."

"And you were the perfect little student," he says. "You never fooled around in class."

"With you guys? All you wanted to do was burp and throw things."

"Still do." Ryan takes a big swig of his drink and burps for emphasis.

I finish my potato chips and reach for another handful. Skippy gets up, opens the window, and lights a cigarette. "I should quit," he says.

"Smoking?" Jenny asks.

"Heck no." He takes a big drag. "Work. Who needs it? All they do is hassle you and make you feel like dirt." He smiles. "I get enough of that at home. Eleven years of schooling—I deserve better than that."

"Twelve if you count kindergarten," Jenny says.

"That's right. Twelve years. That's enough to drive anybody to drinking." He takes another long drag from his smoke. "Anyway, I *am* quitting that job soon. No way I'm spending the rest of my life loading trucks. I got a way bigger future than that."

Wobbly but on Target

They don't waste any time getting the intramural league started. There are six seventh-grade classes, and we'll play each of the other five twice in touch football. The courtyard outside the school is all blacktop; not a blade of grass in sight.

We play Mr. Blaine's class in the opener. The games are at lunchtime, so everybody goes down the block to Chicken Delite or Lovey's Pizza to grab a quick bite beforehand. Then we hustle to the locker room and change into our gym uniforms: baggy gray shorts and blue T-shirts with numbers in a white block. Mine is XS-107. The XS is for "extra small."

Blaine's class has a lot of the smart kids, and I'm surprised I'm not in it. On the other hand, Tony is, so the criteria can't be *all* brains.

There are twelve guys in our class, and we're supposed to play eight at a time. But Douglas Richter has a metal plate in his head, so he's out, and Thomas White says he gets too wheezy.

Fine by me. More playing time. Magrini assigns himself the quarterback position and tells me to play flanker. I look around. Diane is in the huddle.

"You cheering?" Magrini asks her.

"No. Playing."

"Who says you can play?"

"Who says I can't?"

Magrini frowns and shrugs. "Okay." He looks her over. "Play safety." He gives everybody else assignments on either offense or defense or both. I'll be an outside linebacker, too.

Basic rules. Two completions in a row equal a first down, as long as there's forward progress. A touch has to be with two hands. Conversions are worth one point. No field goals, since there aren't any goalposts.

It isn't easy to score. The "field" is about sixty yards long but narrow. And we only have about half an hour for the game. Mr. Eckel, an eighth-grade teacher, is the referee. His eyes are severely crossed, so it's almost impossible to tell if he's talking to you.

The game is scoreless when he says we've got eight more minutes. Blaine's class has the ball and has completed four passes in a row, but they're only a few feet past midfield. Benny Allegretti is the quarterback.

Tony is glaring at me, but he breaks into a smile when I meet his eyes. He's my responsibility. He does a simple square-out and nabs the pass, but I stop him immediately.

"I saw Patty and Janet yesterday," he says, walking back.

"So?"

"Just thought you'd want to know. Patty asked about you."

His teammates start making noise about getting back onside, so he jogs to the huddle. When he splits out again, he's got a bigger smile.

At the snap, he darts three steps forward, stops and makes a half turn toward the sideline, then breaks long. I stumble with the fake and he gets past me.

The pass is wobbly but on target, and Tony's got me by a couple of yards. But Diane steps in front of him as the ball begins to dive, and she picks it off. I meet Tony as he rushes back, blocking him hard. Then I turn and follow Diane, who's sprinting along the sideline. Allegretti is zeroing in on her.

"Behind you!" I shout.

Barely looking back, Diane flips me the ball, and her momentum carries her into Benny, knocking him to the pavement. I catch the ball, hurdle over him, and break into the clear. Nobody gets close, and I race into the end zone.

The team mobs me. "Way to go, Winslow!" Magrini yells, putting me in a bear hug and lifting me off my feet.

We line up for the extra point. Nobody gets open, so Magrini scrambles around until Allegretti gets his hands on him.

"Defense!" we shout. Allegretti panics and throws four long incompletions. We run the ball three times and take our time getting back. Eckel blows his whistle and we jump up and down.

I take a seat under the fire escape and soak it all in.

"Nice run," Diane says, walking over to me.

"Great interception. Heads-up lateral, too."

She pats her chest. "I know what I'm doing," she says. "I've been playing with the boys forever. I have two older brothers."

"Lucky for us," I say.

She sits next to me. The girls' uniforms are blue one-piece things with shorts and mid-arm-length sleeves. No numbers. I guess they step into them and button them up in back.

"Pretty good team," she says.

"Yeah. Magrini has a decent arm."

"I mean you and me. That was real teamwork on the runback."

"Heck of a block," I say.

"I suckered him. You should have heard him cursing under his breath."

I look around to see who's in earshot. "He's a bit of a jerk," I say.

"No kidding. He kept asking me out last year."

Interesting. So she's at that level, popularity-wise. "What'd you say?"

She lifts her eyebrows. "Nothing bad. He wasn't a pest or anything, so I was sort of flattered. But I wasn't attracted, either. I let him down easy. He moved on to other things in a hurry."

"Like what?"

She laughs. "You mean *who*. Debbie Fitzpatrick. Then Donna Egan. I don't remember who came next."

"But you could have been the first."

"Quite an honor."

The early bell rings, so we've got five minutes. We're still in our gym uniforms. I scramble to my feet and start to offer her a hand, but she's already up.

"Race you to the gym," she says. And she starts running before I can react.

I catch her halfway there and look over with a big grin as I pass her. She grits her teeth and opens her mouth like she's putting everything she's got into it, but I can tell she's kidding around. I stop three feet from the gym door and let her get there first.

"See you in class," she says, still running as she reaches the hallway to the locker rooms.

"Wait!" I say. I have no idea why I say it, and I have nothing to say when she stops.

She looks at me like she's waiting for something important.

"I went to Woodstock," I finally say.

She shrugs and smiles. "Cool." And then she goes into the locker room.

I head into the bathroom and run the water until it turns cold, then splash some on my face and wipe it off with the front of my T-shirt. I look at myself in the mirror. Feeling good.

The game-winning touchdown. And great teamwork.

I'm starting to like junior high school.

FRIDAY, SEPTEMBER 5:

Trick Handcuffs

I'm still awake when Ryan comes home from work, watching *The Honeymooners* in the family room with Dad. Mom went to bed an hour ago. It's the one where Ralph and Norton get handcuffed together on the train to the Raccoon convention.

Ryan is wearing that red headband again.

"You didn't work in that thing, did you?" Dad asks.

"No. That'd get me fired." Ryan opens the refrigerator and takes out the pitcher of lemonade. "Of course, that would probably be the best move I could make."

"Getting fired?"

"Sure. Who needs that job anyway?"

Dad gets up from the couch and walks to the kitchen. I stay where I am on the love seat, but I can hear every word they say.

"Listen, buddy. The guy who needs that job is you."

"What for? As if I'm making some great career move by stacking bags of frozen string beans."

"Right. You'd be much better off just watching TV all day."

"That job rots."

"So find a better one. The corporate world is falling all over itself trying to find *high school graduates* like you."

I can hear Ryan pouring the lemonade. There's a pause, then he sets the glass down with a *clink*. "I should travel," he says. "Go see California or something."

"In that car you don't have."

"I could hitch. Or take a bus."

"With that money you're not earning."

"I am earning money."

"Right. By working."

I can hear them glaring at each other. "You don't get it," Ryan says for about the hundredth time this summer.

"Listen," Dad says. "What I get is that it's very easy to think big when you're seventeen and you imagine that your future is unlimited. But you're in total denial, Ryan. September ninth is four days away. The government has a nice birthday present waiting for you. It's called a draft card."

"You think I don't know that?"

"There's been no evidence that you do."

"I'm not buying into their fascist system, Dad."

Dad's voice gets loud now, and very intense. "You bought into it the day you were born, buddy. You're an American. You think I want you going to Vietnam? You think I'm happy that you haven't done a damn thing to avoid that?"

"I *am* doing things, Dad."

"Like what?"

"Like speaking out against this stupid war."

"To who? To Brody? To the back-end losers at Shop-Rite? Tell me who, Ryan. Your genius friend Skippy?"

They're quiet for half a minute. Ryan mutters, "This is a pointless conversation." He comes into the family room and flops down on the couch.

Dad comes, too, but he just stands behind us and stares at the television. Ralph and Norton are now trying to go to sleep in the same bunk, since they can't get the trick handcuffs undone. Usually we'd be laughing our heads off, even though we've seen this episode fifty times. But we all just sit there in silence.

Ryan slowly pulls the headband off and sets it on the coffee table. I catch his eye and he frowns, then lets out a sigh.

I switch the station and we catch the end of the sports report; the Mets split a doubleheader with the Phillies. Then they repeat the top news story of the day: The U.S. Army has brought charges against a lieutenant for the massacre of Vietnamese civilians at My Lai last year.

There's an episode of *The Burns and Allen Show* on channel 11, but we just stare at it for five minutes.

Dad clears his throat. "You know, Ryan, it's admirable when someone stands up for a cause they truly believe in. Martin Luther King, the Kennedys. But it's chicken shit when a kid just sits in a safe environment—Mommy making his dinner every night, Daddy paying the bills—and makes a lot of noise without taking any action. At least—at the very least—you need to get yourself into college as soon as possible and give yourself some cover. There's a real world out there, buddy. Realer than you want to know."

Dad heads upstairs. Ryan lies down and stares at the ceiling. Then he shuts his eyes, and I just look at him for a few minutes. The laugh track on the TV show is going strong, but I don't pay attention. He rubs his eyes.

Ryan sits up and nods at me. I can tell Dad shook him up. He carefully folds the headband into a square. Then he goes back to the kitchen and returns with another glass of lemonade. He uses the folded-up headband as a coaster.

"Did you want anything?" he asks softly.

"No. I'm good."

He nods again and chews gently on his lip. "He's right," he says eventually. "You do have to take action. . . . And I plan to. Just not the way he wants me to."

"What do you mean?"

He shrugs. "I don't know yet. More than just speaking out, I guess. Something that'll make more of a difference."

"Oh."

I should get to bed; we've got another game tomorrow night. But I wouldn't be sleeping anyway, so I'd rather stay here with Ryan. He's been there for me. Teaching me how to shoot a basketball or cook a hot dog. Taking me to the movies, even when he goes to the drive-in with Jenny. Giving me things like a Giants jersey he got too big for, or a flashlight when I was four and scared that there was a monster in my closet.

Now he's scared. I'm scared, too.

We might as well sit here together.

The Mini-Backfield

Our second game is a rare away one at night. It's at Hudson City, which has a lighted field like ours.

On the bus ride over, the cheerleaders go through all the players' names. I brace for my own: "Rah rah Brody Winslow!" I don't think half the cheerleaders even know who I am. I'm not sure any of them do. At least they act like they don't if I pass them in the hallway at school.

Not that I care that much. They're kind of stuck-up. But I seem pretty much invisible to girls on the whole. Except maybe Diane. I'm not invisible to her, but I don't know if I'm just a humorous guy who sits next to her in school or somebody she could get interested in.

Tony nudges me when he hears Stephie doing the cheer for my name. I elbow him back harder. She's going out with Lorenzo, apparently.

Most of the guys are staring out the windows or at the

back of the seats in front of them. Very intense. We heard that Hudson City won big last week. Much bigger than our one-point squeaker. So everybody's quietly getting psyched up.

We'll be kicking off to start the game, so I trot over to the opposite sideline and bounce up and down a few times. Hudson City's in red jerseys and black helmets. You can see the Empire State Building across the river from the field and the high-rises of Jersey City a little ways down the river on this side.

The Hudson City guy across from me is a lot bigger than I am. Mitchell kicks off and I angle away from the sideline, waiting for Sarnoski to pass me. Two Hudson City players move to block him, and I dart past them all and get over to where I'm supposed to be.

I do a perfect box-and-in, but the action is on the other side of the field. Looks like Tony got in on the tackle.

I run to our sideline and join him in front of the bench.

"Totally nailed the guy," Tony says, pulling off his helmet. He heads to the watercooler and gets a cupful. "Saved a touchdown."

Didn't look that way to me. That whole side of the field was well covered. But let him think that if he wants to. It's his first real contribution of the season.

We get back on the field midway through the second quarter after Esposito dives into the end zone. The coaches kept him out of the scrimmages all week to make sure his ankle would heal, and he seems fine now.

This time the returner comes straight up the middle. It's tempting to head toward him, but my job is to protect the sideline. Good thing, too, because his teammates throw a couple of blocks and he turns my way. Sarnoski makes the initial hit, but the guy is still moving forward. I hesitate for a split second, remembering that penalty, but then I throw myself at his waist and wrap both arms around him. He goes down.

My teammates are clapping and yelling as we run off. "Good coverage!" Coach Epstein calls, though not directly at me.

We're up 7–6 at the half—the exact same score as last week's final. Looks like it'll be too close again for me to get any playing time outside of the kickoffs.

But Esposito scores again in the third quarter, and Ferrante scrambles around the end for a touchdown late in the fourth. Still, I'm surprised when Coach says, "Where's that mini-backfield?"

He waves me, Tony, and Salinardi over. "If we hold 'em here and get the ball back, you guys are going in," he says. "Just run the ball and *hold onto it*. Basically, we'll run out the clock."

I try to swallow, but my mouth has turned bone-dry. So I get a cup of water and hold it in there. Then I swallow it, but I'm so nervous it nearly comes back up.

The opportunity comes with 1:19 remaining, after a Hudson City drive stalls at our forty.

"They'll be coming at you with everything they've got," Coach Epstein tells us. "Hold on to that ball."

Salinardi is stuttering in the huddle. This game is probably out of reach, but a major screwup would make things dicey. "Umm . . . twenty . . . no, forty-three," he says. "On two."

That's a handoff to me.

I put my hands on my knees and stare at Tony's back. He'll hit the hole first. All I want to do is gain a couple of yards and kill the clock. Nothing fancy.

Tony lunges to the right. I follow him. But Salinardi pivots to the left. I stop cold. He wraps both arms around the ball and goes down hard.

"What happened?" he says as we huddle up. "Forty-three is to the left!"

I shut my eyes. I know that. But Tony went the wrong way and I stayed behind him. "My fault," I say.

He turns and looks at the clock. Hudson City called time-out as soon as he was tackled, so we've still got 1:08 left.

"Thirty-three," he says. "Tony. To the *left*. On two."

Tony scrambles forward and gets back to the original line of scrimmage. Hudson City calls its final time-out. It's third-and-ten.

Colaneri comes running onto the field, sending Tony off. "Coach says don't pass," he tells Salinardi. "Hand off to Brody."

"Okay," Salinardi says. "Forty-four."

"Follow me," Colaneri says, not looking at me. "We need yards."

The handoff is clean and I hug the ball. I get a nice block from Colaneri and churn through the line. I see daylight to my left, but it closes quickly, so I keep running straight and a linebacker hauls me down.

"Nice run!" Colaneri says, yanking me to my feet. I look over at the sideline and see that I'm halfway between the sticks. So it's fourth-and-five, but now the clock is running.

"Let it go," Colaneri says in the huddle. He's taken over; Salinardi is just listening. "I'll call time-out with about twenty seconds left. Then you just hand off to me. Game over."

So that should be it for me. I line up behind Colaneri, then run behind him as he charges into the line. He picks up seven. First down. The seconds tick off and we celebrate.

"Great win!" Magrini says, running onto the field with his helmet held high.

"Two-and-O, baby!" Ferrante yells. "Out of sight!"

We're rowdy all the way home. Somebody says something about going to Lovey's for pizza. I hate pizza, but I figure we should walk down that way and hang out a while.

Tony's kind of angry. "Why'd he yank me out?" he asks. "I'd just made a huge gain."

The gain was two yards, but that *is* huge compared to a loss. "He had to get a message to Salinardi to keep the ball on the ground," I say. "That's all."

"Yeah, I guess. But he could have taken you out. You're the one who messed up on the first play."

"That's because I was following you."

"I was being a decoy," he says.

"That's not how the play works."

He laughs. "I know. I forgot. But you shouldn't have; you were getting the ball!"

"Just as well," I say. "There was no hole. Joey got clobbered."

Tony shrugs. The bus comes to a stop and we pile off.

"You got money?" Tony asks.

"I got a dollar in my sock."

"Buy me a soda at least?"

"Sure."

We duck into the Garden State store and get two cans of 7UP. By the time we reach Lovey's, it's full. So we just stand outside—not exactly part of the scene, but not totally removed from it, either.

I keep thinking about my run. First official carry of my career. Five yards. A statistic nobody can ever take away from me.

We watch the constant stream of cars and buses for about twenty minutes, just sipping our 7UP and leaning against the front of the pizza place.

"Had enough?" Tony asks.

"Yeah." I look into Lovey's. Every table is full, most of them with football players and cheerleaders. They're all laughing and eating.

We head up the Boulevard toward home. The buildings are dark now except for Lovey's, Chicken Delite, and the Limerick Tavern on the corner.

We don't say much on the way home. But I'm thinking.

So far so good, I suppose.

SUNDAY, SEPTEMBER 7

What They're Saying

By Brody Winslow

Dylan asks, "How many roads?"
My dad sees a headband on a coward.
The Youngbloods tell me, "Fear's the way we die."
My brother sees misuse of power.
My dad mentions King and Kennedy and Yogi.
Sly sings he's no better "and neither are you."
My brother says it's time to make a difference.
The Archies describe the loveliness of loving you.
My mom says she'll drive to Toronto.
The Beatles hint of Paul so we'll grieve for him.
My brother could be a walrus, too.
The cheerers chant rah rah; we believe 'em.

MONDAY, SEPTEMBER 8:

Like a John Tunis Novel

Me and Ryan can't even sit down, pacing back and forth in the family room. The Mets are clinging to a one-run lead over the Cubs, who've started slumping just as the Mets have caught fire. If the Mets can hold on to this one, they'll be inches away from first place.

First place! This is the Mets we're talking about.

Top of the ninth. One out. Shea Stadium is rocking. I stuff a handful of pretzels into my mouth.

"It's late!" Mom yells from the top of the stairs.

"This is the greatest baseball game ever!" Ryan calls back.

"Brody needs to get to bed!"

I roll my eyes and shake my head. "Two more minutes!" I yell, hoping she'll close her door and go to sleep. Koosman is two outs away from finishing this thing.

He gets his thirteenth strikeout. Ryan throws out five quick punches, gritting his teeth. "Dig it!" he says.

"Unreal."

"It's almost ten o'clock!" Mom yells.

I can't even look. I walk out to the kitchen and open the refrigerator. There's a pitcher of watery lemonade, a few slices of leftover bacon from this morning on a paper plate, and a half-eaten chicken breast. Plus all the stuff in jars, like olives and pickles and mustard.

"It's over!" Ryan yells. I sprint the eight feet to the family room, where Ryan is dancing around, punching at the air again.

"I am stoked!" he says. "Seaver's pitching tomorrow night and I'm off. We're going!"

"We're going?"

"You better believe we are. What time do you get done with football?"

"About five thirty."

"I'll pick you up at the field. You can change in the car."

"We're really going?"

"We're going!"

I can hear Dad walking down the stairs. "Where are you going?" he asks.

Ryan is kneeling on the couch now, bouncing up and down. "Shea Stadium. Tomorrow night. I can use the car, right?"

Dad tightens his mouth. Mom is right behind him, tying her bathrobe. "You want to take *another* trip?" she asks.

"Just into the city," Ryan replies. "We'd never make it in time on the bus. By the time he gets home from practice and gets changed . . ."

"Can't you go on a Saturday?" she asks. "I'll make sand-wiches."

"Mom, this game is huge. The Cubs. The Mets are a game and a half back and Seaver's pitching. It's like a John Tunis novel come to life."

She purses her lips and turns to Dad, but she doesn't ask his opinion this time. "Brody has school the next morning."

"It's my birthday!" Ryan says. "And we'll be home by nine thirty. Ten at the absolute latest. He can sleep in the car on the way home."

"What about his homework?"

I almost never bring homework home. "I'll get it done between classes or at lunchtime," I say. "Please, Mom. This is the biggest sporting event of my life. You know how bad the Mets have always been. The Yankees and the Giants stink, too."

"This is history!" Ryan says. "The worst team in sports is becoming the best."

Mom and Dad look at each other.

"Haven't you had enough 'history' lately?" Dad asks.

"I brought him back safe from Woodstock," Ryan says. "And this is a lot closer to home."

Mom folds her arms. "Brody is already up too late tonight. By tomorrow night he'd be a wreck."

"No way, Mom," I say. "I'm up past midnight every night."

"Since when?"

"I don't know. A while."

"You can't sleep?"

"I can sleep; I just don't. I listen to the radio."

Ryan laughs. "Sugar, Sugar."

"What?" Mom looks at him like he's speaking Italian.

"Mom," he says, "the man is getting in touch with his emotions."

"The *man* is only twelve."

"He's an *old* twelve. I promise, Jenny will look out for him."

"And Skippy will, too, I suppose?"

"Can't hurt."

Dad clears his throat again and looks directly at me. "Do you *want* to go, Jehosaphat, or are you being dragged along again so Ryan can justify another trip?"

"I definitely want to go, Dad. I've never been to Shea, *remember*?" He's threatened to take me several times, but it never happens. I can detect a trace of guilt in his eyes. Maybe he feels bad about yelling at Ryan the other night, too.

"Okay," he says, not even waiting for Mom to chime in. He points at Ryan. "Straight in and straight out. If you're going to be one *second* later than ten o'clock, you find a pay phone and call us."

"You got it," Ryan says.

"I'll make sandwiches anyway," Mom says softly. She gives me a hard look. "You bring a jacket. It can get cold very quickly this time of year."

TUESDAY, SEPTEMBER 9:

Everyday People

Coach gathers us after the wind sprints for a pep talk. Everybody's gasping for breath except me. I can't even stand still, stepping from foot to foot and wishing he would finish. Ryan, Skippy, and Jenny are already waiting in the parking lot.

"So don't be getting big heads just because you've won a couple of games," Coach is saying. He picks at a side tooth with his thumbnail. "Over-confidence is a killer. You go into a game thinking you're a big deal and you'll come out with a loss, feeling like a bunch of crapheads. . . . So we'll see you on the field tomorrow, ready to work."

I sprint across the field and up the hill into the parking lot, then climb into the backseat next to Skippy. There's a Mets pennant on the seat.

Ryan reaches over and holds out a hand for me to slap. "Brody boy! You ready for this?"

"You kidding? I couldn't think of anything else all day."

I turn and watch the other players walking slowly off the field. Tony's by himself.

We drive up to the Boulevard and turn right.

"Which way you going?" I ask.

"Skippy forgot his wallet," Ryan says. "So we gotta stop there."

Skippy lives on the other side of town, so that'll cost us some time. But we ought to get to Shea in about forty minutes. It's around quarter to six now. Game time is 7:05.

We pass Corpus Christi and I see Patty and Janet on the steps. *Waiting for somebody?* I wonder.

I pull my jersey and shoulder pads over my head, then untie my sneakers. My T-shirt is soaked, but there's a fresh one and a pair of dungarees in a paper Shop-Rite bag, plus a sweatshirt with a hood.

Jenny looks back and smiles. "I won't watch," she says.

So I yank off the football pants and the cup and put the dungarees on in a hurry.

"Whoa," Skippy says. "Those socks stink."

I peel one off and smell it. It's wet and ripe, but there aren't any fresh ones in the bag. So I ball them up, stick them inside my helmet, and put my bare feet back in my sneakers.

"You think we'll get good tickets?" I ask.

"Sure," Ryan answers. "We'll probably be in the upper deck, but all the seats at Shea are good. It'll be packed, I can tell you that much."

Ryan keeps the station wagon running while we wait in front of Skippy's house. Something else must be going on in there, because he's gone for fifteen minutes.

"Look what Jenny got me for my birthday," Ryan says, handing a record album over the seat.

It's *Stand!* Sly and the Family Stone.

"Cool," I say. I've been hearing some of this on the radio lately, like "Everyday People."

Skippy finally comes back with a cigarette between his lips and a can of soda. "What a hassle," he says, frowning toward his house.

"Your old man home?" Ryan asks.

"Home and wasted," he says. "Wanted me to wash his car. Tonight. Can you believe that?"

"What'd you say?" Jenny asks.

"I said to wash his own stupid car. I'll do it tomorrow."

It's way after six by the time we get on Route 80, heading toward the George Washington Bridge. Traffic is heavy. "We'll make it," Ryan says. "We can catch the first inning on the radio if we have to."

"So, Brody," Jenny says, leaning partway over the seat, "you hear about tomorrow night?"

"No."

Jenny always treats me like I'm an equal, like I'm part of the gang. She's the kind of girlfriend I'd want to have if I ever got one.

"We're going to a war protest," she says.

"In town?"

"In *our* town? You kidding?" She laughs. "Up in Syracuse. At my cousin's college."

"Oh. You off again tomorrow, Ryan?"

Ryan shakes his head. "I'm off for real tonight. Tomorrow I'm calling in sick."

"Again?"

He fake-coughs. "You get a lot of bronchitis in that stupid freezer."

"It's gonna be so great," Jenny says. "Very peaceful. A bunch of people are just getting together in front of the student center and reading the names of the war dead and holding candles. It's basically a vigil to get the military recruiters off the campus. We'll be there until sunrise."

"With big signs," Skippy says.

"Small signs," Jenny says. "Just making a point about non-violence. And screwing the government."

"You using the car again, Ryan?"

"Nope. We're catching a ride with Jenny's other cousin from Jersey City."

"Dad know?"

"Dad doesn't need to know. But I will tell you this: I'm taking action."

"We're taking big-time action," Skippy says.

"Peaceful action," Jenny repeats.

"Maybe you," Skippy says. "I'm gonna make enough noise to get this war ended."

We've reached Englewood, but the road ahead looks very congested. We've been listening to WMCA, so Ryan switches the channel, looking for a traffic report.

He finds the Mets pregame, and we listen to that for a few minutes, barely moving forward. It's Tom Seaver versus Ferguson Jenkins tonight, two of the best pitchers in the league. The Cubs have lost five straight, and the Mets have won three in a row and nineteen of their last twenty-five.

People in other cars are holding up Mets pennants and beeping their horns when we hold up ours. But we're at a standstill now, and we're still a couple of miles from the bridge.

Ryan finally finds a traffic report. There's at least one accident ahead of us, and one lane of the bridge is closed, but it turns out that this is mostly Mets traffic. Everybody in New Jersey decided they couldn't possibly miss this game.

There's not much we can do. We're not near an exit, so we just wait it out. Ryan shuts off the engine.

"You bring me some food?" I ask.

Jenny hands me a small paper bag with two peanut butter sandwiches and a can of lemon soda. There's no can opener, though. I drank a lot of water toward the end of practice, so I'll be okay. I eat the sandwiches.

Through three innings, Seaver has a perfect game going, so I can just imagine what it'd be like to actually be there. Donn Clendenon hits a two-run homer in the bottom of the third, giving the Mets a 4–0 lead.

We've inched forward about sixty feet since the game started. A few cars have cut across the grass median and headed back the other way, but there are cop cars over there now.

"This is ridiculous," Skippy says, lighting another cigarette.

Ryan smiles. "What's Yogi Berra say? 'It's déjà vu all over again.' But hey, we made it to Woodstock."

"Woodstock went all night," Skippy replies.

"That it did."

The perfect game gets busted in the fourth, but Seaver himself hits a leadoff double in the bottom of the inning and later scores.

Ryan turns off the engine again. People have gotten out of some of the cars around us and are drinking beers. Everybody has the game on full volume, so we get out, too. Skippy bums a beer from somebody. We lean against the car and enjoy our second major traffic jam of the summer, laughing and cheering after almost every pitch. Everything's going right for the Mets.

By the time Jerry Grote hits an RBI double in the seventh, the Mets seem to have it on ice. A cop waves us across the median, and suddenly we're going 55 again, heading for home.

Dad's not real pleased when he hears about the adventure. He's standing in the kitchen with his arms folded while we tell him.

"I'm surprised you didn't abandon the car again and walk to the stadium."

Ryan frowns. "We would have, but we didn't have any Tang."

Dad turns and faces Mom. "That's typical Ryan. Six miles from his destination."

"What did you expect us to do, Dad? I mean, has it *ever* been hard to get to a Mets game before?"

"You could have left earlier."

"Brody had football practice."

"Then you could have stayed home. But you haven't learned that lesson, have you?"

"What lesson? I'm not going to spend my life afraid to do stuff. You think reading about things the next day or watching them on TV is the same as being there?"

"It's better than *not* being there," Dad says. "What'd you gain tonight? You missed the whole stupid game. When you went to that ridiculous Woodstock thing, you did more walking than watching. How smart was that?"

Ryan lets out a huge sigh. "You don't get it."

"You got that right. I don't."

Ryan sets the keys on the counter and shakes his head. "Here's the car. No harm done." He points to me. "Brody's home safe and sound. And guess what, Dad? We had a blast."

Dad snorts and looks at Mom again. "'A blast,' he says. Sitting on Route 80 for two hours is his idea of a good time.

Hey, here's an idea. You like driving so much, maybe you can get a job as a truck driver."

"Wouldn't be so bad," Ryan says.

"Or a tank driver," Dad says. He raises his eyebrows. "You fill out those college papers?"

Ryan frowns deeper and shakes his head. "I will."

"You better." Dad picks up the keys and puffs out his cheeks. He fixes his eyes on me for the first time. "Nehemiah," he says. "You better get to bed. . . . We all should."

Mom and Dad start up the stairs. I look at Ryan and we both hold back a laugh.

"Ryan," Dad says. "No more stunts, huh? Starting tomorrow, it's time to get yourself on track."

Ryan waits until he hears their bedroom door click shut. "Tomorrow this time, I'll be in Syracuse."

WEDNESDAY, SEPTEMBER 10:

Ducks in Order

WMCA's counting down the new top ten tonight, so I lie in bed with the light off and look out the window. Here's the list so far:

10. "Sweet Caroline" (Neil Diamond). Good song, but I've had enough of it.

9. "Hot Fun in the Summertime" (Sly and the Family Stone). Cool.

8. "Green River" (Creedence Clearwater Revival). Okay.

7. "I'd Wait a Million Years" (The Grass Roots). Also okay.

6. "I Can't Get Next to You" (The Temptations). Good.

5. "A Boy Named Sue" (Johnny Cash). Hilarious and cool.

4. "I'll Never Fall in Love Again" (Tom Jones). Okay.

Coach Epstein said today that he's hoping the substitutes will get "significant" playing time Saturday night. Wallington has a small team, and they've lost their first two games by about thirty points apiece. So the plan is to play the starters at the beginning, build up a lead, and then let the rest of us get a chance.

I'll believe it when I see it, but it would be cool to get some action other than in the final minute.

First there's this stupid school dance on Friday night. Why would I agree to go to another dance? Tony made me buy a ticket this afternoon. He says some kids from Corpus Christi are going to show up, so we might get another chance with Patty and Janet.

Like I ever want to go through that again.

Number three on the radio is "Jean," which I kind of like but have heard too many times. I can't figure out what number two is going to be. "Honky Tonk Women" has been at the top for four straight weeks with no end in sight.

But after a commercial I hear the familiar sound of the Rolling Stones. They've dropped to second! I keep running down the past few weeks' top songs in my head, but I have no idea what could be number one, unless "Get Together" has made a big comeback. That has to be it! My favorite song of all time!

I run to the bathroom and brush my teeth. For the heck of it, I step onto the scale. I'm up to ninety for the first time in my life. I peel off my T-shirt and flex in front of the mirror. Looking good.

When I get back to the bedroom, I can't believe my ears. It's "Sugar, Sugar" by the Archies. At the top of the charts. All the way up from thirteen a week ago, where I was certain it had peaked.

Life is just unfair sometimes. "Get Together" never made it past number three.

I jolt awake when I hear the phone ringing. Dad picks it up in his and Mom's bedroom and says hello. He listens for a minute, then speaks very softly, so I can't make out what he's saying. But I do hear it when he slams the phone down a few minutes later.

"That idiot!" Dad says.

I turn on my light and step into the hall. Their bedroom door is open, and I can see Dad pulling a pair of pants on over his pajamas.

"He got arrested," Dad says.

"Oh my!" Mom replies. "Where is he?"

"Way up in Syracuse."

"What? I thought he was sleeping at Skippy's."

"Apparently not. They went to some protest. A *war* protest! Why not just invite the government to throw him on the front lines?"

"Are you . . . are you driving all the way up there?"

"No," he says sarcastically, "I thought I'd go for a pleasant ride in the country in the middle of the night. . . . Of course I'm driving up there. Who the hell else is going to bail him out?"

"Do you want me to go with you?"

"No, you better stay with Brody. Is there gas in the car?"

"I think it's three-quarters full."

Dad looks at his watch. "I guess that'll get me there. That lunatic."

I step into the bedroom. "What's going on?"

Dad looks at me for a moment. "Nothing," he says gently. "You can go back to bed."

"Is Ryan in jail?" I ask.

Dad looks at Mom, then takes a deep breath. "He shoved a policeman."

"Is Jenny there, too?" Mom asks.

"Apparently. She's sitting in the police station, waiting. Skippy disappeared, so thank *God* we don't have to worry about him."

Mom makes a scolding sound with her tongue. "Skippy's just a kid."

"So was Billy."

Mom looks puzzled. "Billy who?"

"Billy the Kid."

I follow them downstairs. It's almost one o'clock. Mom plugs in the coffeepot, and Dad eats two doughnuts while he waits for the coffee to boil. "I'll take it with me," he says. "Do we have anything I can put it in that won't spill?"

Mom searches a cabinet and takes out an old plaid thermos.

Dad shakes his head. "What a palooka."

"He's only eighteen," Mom says.

"I'll eighteen him." He wipes some doughnut dust off his chest. He's wearing his white work shirt from yesterday; I saw him fish it out of the hamper.

"Drive carefully," Mom says. "There's no reason to hurry."

"It's a four-hour drive," Dad says. "By the time I get there, they'll probably be fitting him in battle fatigues. Or prison gear."

"Don't say that," Mom replies.

"Well, what do you think? They'll throw a guy like Muhammad Ali in jail, but just wave off some stupid kid and give him a birthday cake? This is serious stuff."

Mom sniffs hard. "I know it is."

"If you're gonna protest the war, you'd better have your ducks in order," Dad says. "No college, no credentials, and he has the audacity to get himself arrested."

Dad leans against the kitchen door and shuts his eyes. Mom's crying. He sighs and walks over to her, and they hug hard for a minute.

"It'll be all right," Dad whispers. "It'll be all right." He kisses her on the forehead. "Call my office in the morning and tell them I should be in by noon."

Dad puts an arm around my shoulder and pulls me toward him. "Get some sleep, Brody," he says. "This is gonna be okay. Your brother is a horse's ass, but I don't want you worrying."

"I won't."

Like heck I won't. But what am I supposed to do?

Just wait, I guess.

No way I can sleep. I lie in bed and listen to the radio, worried about Ryan. The war is raging.

I switch to a sports talk show. A caller is going on and on about why the Giants should fire their coach and get a new quarterback. They finally cut the guy off and announce the real news. The Mets swept a doubleheader from the Expos and are in first place.

Unbelievable, but I can't even get excited about it.

I don't want to lose my brother.

THURSDAY, SEPTEMBER 11:

Let Freedom Ring

Mrs. Wilkey is droning on about adjectives and adverbs. I look at the clock. 11:38. Seven more minutes of this and the agony will be over.

There was still no word from Dad when I left for school this morning, but Mom said not to worry. They'd certainly be home before I got back for lunch. At least she hoped so. It all depended. She didn't say on what.

I glance over at Diane. She seems to be taking a lot of notes. I catch her gaze, and she lifts her eyebrows, then looks up at Mrs. Wilkey, who has her back to us while she writes on the blackboard.

Diane tilts her notebook toward me. In big letters it says, *Mrs. Wilkey's ADJECTIVES: fat, ugly, old, BORING!!!!!!*

She underlines *BORING!!!!!!* and smiles at me.

When the bell rings I open my desk and shove my notebook inside. Everybody stands and starts pushing toward the door in a huge hurry to get out.

Diane nudges me with her elbow. "You going to the dance tomorrow night?" she asks.

"Probably," I say. "Yeah."

"Me, too."

"Should be okay."

"Yeah. Should be."

Mrs. Wilkey is sitting at her desk, biting into a jelly sandwich. A couple of people are still fumbling with their stuff at their desks, but mostly it's just me and Diane standing there. I get the feeling that she likes that it's only me and her, but maybe not. Talking about the dance makes me nervous, as if there might be some expectations about actually dancing with her.

"I gotta leave," I say.

She shrugs. "Me, too."

Then again, hanging out with her at the dance might be cool. "I mean, my brother's in jail," I say. "Or he was. I gotta go see."

She points toward the windows at the back of the room, in the direction of the Municipal Building across the street. "Over there?" she asks.

"No. Up in Syracuse." It sounds a lot more important than being in the town jail, like Otis in Mayberry.

"Hope he's all right," she says.

"Should be. I guess." I'm an inch or so taller than she is. Her hair is dark, shiny, and straight, and it's parted down the middle and held back in a black hair band.

"So," she says, "see you after lunch."

"Right. After lunch."

I run the seven blocks and get home in about three minutes. The car isn't in the driveway.

"What's going on?" I say as I enter the kitchen.

Mom smiles at me. "Your father called after you left. Ryan's all right. But I don't know why they haven't gotten home yet. Should be any minute."

She sets a hamburger and some string beans in front of me at the counter, but I don't feel like eating. I just stare at the plate. She sits on Dad's stool, sipping coffee.

And then we hear the car pulling into the driveway. We leap up and look out the window as Dad and Ryan step out. I swallow and sniff back a tear.

She hugs Ryan and cries a little. Then she lets him go and turns to Dad. "Honey, where've you been?"

"We stopped off in Madison."

"Madison? That's not even on the way."

Dad looks at Ryan. "Tell her."

Ryan shrugs. "He dragged me to the admissions office at Drew. I applied in person for January."

"Oh, Ryan," Mom says. "I'm so glad."

"Yeah, well, it's not like I had much choice."

"You had a choice," she says. "You made the right one."

Ryan sits at the counter and puts his head down.

"Are you fellas hungry?" Mom asks.

Ryan lifts his head. "Starving."

Mom throws a couple more hamburgers into the pan.

Dad grabs another doughnut. "Guess I'll shower and get on the bus," he says. He yawns and shakes his head. "They dropped the charges, by the way. Just as long as he never gets in trouble in Syracuse again."

"Like I'd ever go back there," Ryan says.

"Or anywhere else," Dad says. "No more of this protest nonsense, right?"

"No more fighting with the pigs," Ryan says. "But nobody's shutting me up. First amendment says I can protest all I want."

Dad lets out a big sigh. "Let freedom ring." He turns to go up the stairs. We hear him mutter, "What an imbecile."

I sit next to Ryan and pull my plate over, taking a bite of my hamburger. It's gone cold, so I get the ketchup out of the refrigerator and drench it.

"What exactly happened, Ryan?" Mom asks.

"All we were doing was sitting with a crowd of people on the steps of the student center," he says. "At midnight the campus police told us we had to leave, but we said we had a right to be there. They said we didn't. Next thing we know the city police are there, too, pushing people around. I stepped in front of Jenny when one of them got too close. The cop was harassing her. He yells at me to back off. I go 'Get out of my face and leave her alone!' Then I don't know what happened. I wound up pushing the cop. He twisted my arms behind my back and put handcuffs on me."

"Let me see." Mom grabs his hands and inspects his wrists.

"It was nothing, Mom."

"Did they take you away in a police car?"

"Yeah. A whole bunch of us. I was never actually in jail, just in this holding area until they let me use the phone."

"And you're sure they dropped the charges?"

Ryan shrugs. "I don't think they ever charged me with anything. Just wrote down my driver's license information and asked me if I was a student there."

"And what about Jenny?"

"Somebody drove her to the police station. We have no idea where Skippy took off to. He was at the protest for about two seconds. Probably found somebody to get drunk with."

"That's our boy," Mom says.

"Yeah." Ryan laughs. "Somehow I don't think his heart was entirely behind the protest effort."

Mom shakes her head. "Wait until *he* turns eighteen. He didn't even finish high school."

"Nice campus, though," Ryan says. "Drew, I mean. The other one was nice, too. But . . ." He lifts one hand, then the other, like he's comparing the weight of two items. "'Nam, Madison. 'Nam, Madison." He sets his head on the counter again. "I'm exhausted. I'm crashing all afternoon."

"Don't you have to be at work at four?" she asks.

He shuts his eyes. "Aw, geez. . . . I guess so."

"Your father's been up all night, too," Mom says. "Don't ever forget that. Say all you want about his politics, but he's there for you, Ryan. Every step of the way, he's there."

"I know. Believe me, I was scared to death last night. The best thing I've ever seen was him walking into that police station at five o'clock in the morning. Best thing I've ever seen in my life."

Dad comes down a little while later, showered, shaved, and dressed in a business suit. He nods at Ryan and gives him a tight smile. "All in a night's work," he says.

"Yeah," Ryan says. "Thanks."

Dad frowns and pats his own cheek with his palm. Then he clears his throat. "That was . . . brave," he says, "defending Jenny like that." He looks at his watch. "I don't even know the bus schedule for this time of day. Oh well, can't be too long."

"Wait up," I say. I've got twenty minutes before I need to be back at school. "I'll walk down with you."

"Sounds good." He hands me his briefcase and we leave the house together.

All in a night's work.

FRIDAY, SEPTEMBER 12:

A Moment's Sunlight

Tony comes by around quarter to seven. Mom sends him up to my room. I just showered, and I'm trying to figure out what shirt to wear to the dance.

Tony's wearing his practice jersey. It's extremely baggy without the shoulder pads, and he's got the sleeves rolled up. He smells like cologne. He sits on my bed and tells me to hurry.

"It takes two minutes to walk there," I say. The Franklin School gym is small and creaky, so they're having the dance at Euclid. It's just for seventh and eighth graders, though.

"I want to walk up the Boulevard a ways," he says.

"What for?"

"See if we see them."

"Why waste our time?"

He stands and closes my door. "Somebody told me Patty said you were okay after all."

"Who did?"

"I forget."

"What'd they say?"

"Just that she thinks you're a good guy."

"So what does that mean?"

"It means we should take advantage of the situation while we can."

I think I've heard that before. And it backfired. Tony didn't hear anything; I guarantee it.

My practice jersey is filthy, and it's damp from this afternoon. "I can't wear that," I say.

"Suit yourself. But it's a big advantage."

"How?"

"It just is."

I put on a blue button-down shirt that I usually wear to church. We head down my block and turn onto the Boulevard. Sure enough, we get five blocks and see them coming toward us.

Tony smacks my arm. "Act cool. Like this is no big deal."

"Okay."

Janet gives a timid wave as we approach. Patty looks half defiant and half welcoming. They stop on the sidewalk in front of the Pork Store.

"You guys going the wrong way?" Patty asks.

Tony lifts his hand and opens his palm. "We're in no hurry."

Patty juts her head in the general direction of Euclid, back the way we came. "We're going to the dance."

"Us, too."

She smirks and starts walking up the hill toward Burton Avenue, which runs parallel to the Boulevard. That's the street Euclid is on. Tony falls in next to her. I walk with Janet, a few sidewalk squares behind.

"Hope this is better than that swim club dance," Janet says.

I feel myself blushing. "At least there won't be all those older people."

Tony seems comfortable with Patty. I'm not sure what they're talking about, but he's doing most of it and she's been laughing some.

"So," I say to Janet. "Um . . . how's Corpus Christi?"

"Fine. How's Franklin?"

"Different. It feels, I don't know, like being cut off from something."

"What do you mean?"

"Seven years at Euclid. Not that I miss it, but it's like there's no safety net at Franklin. Nobody knows you. At Euclid you'd see your second-grade teacher in the hallway. . . . I don't know. It's just different."

She nods. "I know what you mean, I think. I've been at CC since first grade."

We get to Burton and turn right. This street is lined with trees and houses, much different from the Boulevard, which is all stores and banks and offices. We walk in the street because there's no traffic and it just seems cool to be off the sidewalk.

A block from the school, Tony and Patty stop so we can

catch up to them; we'd fallen about thirty yards behind. I can see a crowd near the entrance. And I see Diane among them. We lock eyes for just a second, then she looks away and walks into the school. I feel a chill in my gut. How does this look, showing up with these two?

There are folding chairs lining both sides of the gym, and a band made up of high schoolers is on the stage. Three guitarists and a drummer.

Mostly it's girls on one side of the gym and boys on the other, with a large mixed group standing near the stage. Patty and Janet put their jackets on a chair on the boys' side and look around. Tony starts to walk toward some guys from the football team (half of them have their jerseys on), but Patty grabs his arm and pulls him back.

I look around, too. I see Diane staring at us from the opposite corner of the gym. She turns away again.

The band starts. About eight girls start dancing on one side of the basketball court, and about six guys—all of them eighth graders—on the other. Eventually Magrini and Esposito and some other seventh-grade guys start, too, plus most of the cheerleaders. But no guys are dancing with girls.

Patty and Janet kind of dance in place, just moving their shoulders a little. I sit on one of the folding chairs.

When the third song starts—the Stones' "Satisfaction"—Tony reaches for Janet's hand and they go out to the center of the basketball court. Two other couples are dancing now, too.

Patty gives me a challenging look and points her thumb

toward them. Then she breaks into a huffy laugh and tilts her head like she's asking me a question. I feel light-headed and scrawny, but I follow her out there and start dancing, basically trying to copy what Tony's doing.

I feel like everybody's watching me make a fool of myself, but when I look around nobody is. By the time the song ends, about half the people in the gym are dancing. Patty hasn't looked at me once.

They start a slow one—"Crimson and Clover"—and just about everybody heads to the sidelines. Tony stays out there with Janet and puts his arms around her shoulders, rocking back and forth.

I sit down again. Patty doesn't. She continues that swaying stuff. Some eighth-grade girls come over and start talking to her, all bubbly and excited. When the next song starts, she steps onto the floor with them, dancing in a group. I stay where I am.

Within five minutes she's dancing with Magrini.

Tony and Janet haven't stopped yet. She appears to be teaching him some dance moves as they go.

I see Diane walk across the gym toward the exit and I get up before I can think about it and follow her. I let out a sigh of relief when I see her go into the girls' room instead of leaving the building.

I wait. When she comes out I go, "Hi! When did you get here?" as if I hadn't seen her before. Then I remember that we'd locked eyes outside, so that must sound pretty lame.

She's wearing a thin silver chain with a peace sign around her neck. She smiles and says, "A little while ago. I saw you come in."

"Oh. Yeah, I was . . . Tony made me . . . be late."

One corner of her mouth turns up. "He's quite the dancer."

"Yeah."

"You, too, huh?"

I look down and my face gets hot, but it's just embarrassment. "Not really."

"You looked good," she says. "She . . . uh—"

"No." I shake my head. "She's just . . . Tony's with her friend. You know?"

She shrugs gently. "Sure. I get it."

We walk into the gym and stand off to the side of the stage, watching the band. The drummer lives down the block from me and is on the high school track team. Sometimes I see him running sprints up the hill. Two of the guitarists are always sitting in Lovey's Pizza, staring out at the traffic.

Diane is doing that same shoulder-swaying thing. I swallow hard, knowing that I should ask her to dance, but it turns out I don't have to. We just face each other and start moving at the same time. But they're playing a Beatles song that's hard to dance to because it's slow and jerky, so it forces you to exaggerate your movements and then hold them for a split second. She's smiling at me a lot, though. I start laughing.

Then they do "Everyday People," which is a thousand times more fun to dance to. We get cups of soda after that one and sit on the folding chairs and watch the band some more.

"You learn those dance moves at Woodstock?" she asks with a laugh.

I can feel my face turning red. "I guess," I say. "Some of 'em."

The dance ends at nine thirty. I don't even look around for Tony.

"I'll walk you home," I say.

"Great." Diane waves her hand to our right. "I live on Central." Nine blocks from here.

Everybody's leaving at once, so the sidewalks are packed. We joke around about stuff. She says the boys are lucky to be taking shop. "Home Ec is so lame. Half these girls can't even sew on a button. I'd much rather be using a coping saw."

"Really? I'd rather be knitting."

She laughs. "Maybe I can teach you."

"No thanks."

The crowd has thinned a lot by the time we pass Franklin, so we slow down. Then we stand in front of her house for a couple of minutes and talk about the dance, how some of the oddest couples turned up on the floor.

"So I'll see you later," she says, glancing over her shoulder at the house, which has a lot of lights on. I saw her father looking out a window a minute ago.

"Right," I say.

She turns and walks up the driveway. I wait until she's in, then I start running. Suddenly I have tons of energy.

I cut back along Burton, but I see a crowd of kids coming toward me, a block away. Tony and Magrini are among them, with Patty and Janet. Maybe Tony's ready for that group, but I don't need 'em. I turn down to Terrace and run that way toward home. It's very dark. I feel great. I start sprinting and go an extra two blocks past home, then circle back. I could keep running all night, but I'll save it.

I go straight to bed and listen to the radio until way after midnight. I hear "Sugar, Sugar" three times and "Little Woman" twice. I still can't stand the Archies, but the Bobby Sherman song is like a virus in my head that I can't shake.

Blah, blah blah.

It turns out that the Mets swept a doubleheader from the Pirates today, a pair of 1–0 victories. That's nine wins in a row, and they're already extending their lead in the division.

Big game for me tomorrow night. If the Mets can go from worst to first, then I can triumph, too. Diane said she'd be there.

Finally they play "Get Together." I relax and sing along very, very softly. "We are but a moment's sunlight, fading in the grass. . . ."

I hear Ryan come in and open the refrigerator. Then he walks quietly up the stairs and shuts his door across the hallway from me. A few minutes later he knocks gently on mine and I say, "Come in."

"What's happening, man?" he whispers. "You still awake?"

"Yeah."

"How'd the dance go?"

I push up on one elbow. Every light in the house is off. "It was all right," I say. "I had fun."

"Just thought I'd check."

"Thanks. It was good."

"Peace out, then. See you in the morning."

"You, too."

He steps into the hallway, but I call him back.

"Ryan?"

"Yeah?"

"Did it work? The protest in Syracuse?"

"I don't know." He takes another step into the room. "I haven't heard if we had any luck getting the recruiters off campus. But yeah, I think it worked . . . in a small way. Every voice makes a difference. Some are just louder than others. . . . Some people are a lot braver than I am."

He closes the door. I turn off the radio and very quietly try to sing myself to sleep.

> *Come on people now*
> *Smile on your brother*
> *Everybody get together*
> *Try to love one another right now.*

Tomorrow night could be huge. I can see it clearly: The starters build up a reasonable lead in the first half, and me and Tony and Joey take over the backfield for the second.

We begin a drive, keeping the ball on the ground, hitting the holes for four, five yards at a crack, piling up the first downs. I'm sweating and my heart is pounding, but I'm confident. I'm not screwing up anymore.

We cross midfield, into their territory, but then maybe we stall. Tony loses a yard. It's third-and-eight, and Joey looks around the huddle. He locks eyes with me.

"Forty-six pitch," he says.

We break the huddle. I stare straight ahead and take a deep breath, hands on my knees. The lights are on and the bleachers are full, and all eyes are on us.

Joey flips me the football, and I hear the crack of the shoulder pads as the linemen ram into each other. I see that hole opening up. I see me bursting through it, hugging the ball and cutting toward the sideline.

A linebacker angles toward me, but I shift my weight and dodge past him, stiff-arming him and breaking free. I hear the coaches and the spectators yelling. I hear the defenders running toward me.

I'm in a full sprint now, heading up the sideline, ahead of everyone as I race toward the end zone.

I see nothing but daylight ahead.